Burned

a novel

Other books in the Soul Surfer Series:

Nonfiction:

Body & Soul
Rise Above: A 90-Day Devotional
Ask Bethany, Updated Edition

Fiction:

Clash (Book One)
Burned (Book Two)
Storm (Book Three)
Crunch (Book Four)

a novel

By Rick Bundschuh
Inspired by Bethany Hamilton

ZONDERKIDZ

Burned
Copyright © 2007 by Bethany Hamilton
Illustrations © 2007 by Taia Morley

Requests for information should be addressed to:
Zonderkidz, 3900 *Sparks Dr., Grand Rapids, Michigan* 49546

This edition: 978-0-310-74555-6

Library of Congress Cataloging-in-Publication Data

Bundschuh, Rick, 1951-
    Burned / by Rick Bundschuh; inspired by Bethany Hamilton.
       p. cm.— (Soul surfer series)
    Summary: On a surfing vacation with her family in Samoa, fourteen-year-old
Bethany Hamilton has a run-in with an arrogant, angry young man and discovers
a Samoan tradition that brings healing and forgiveness.
    ISBN 978-0-310-71223-7 (softcover)
    1. Hamilton, Bethany—Juvenile fiction. [1. Hamilton, Bethany—Fiction. 2.
Surfing—Fiction. 3. Christian life—Fiction. 4.Amputees—Fiction. 5. People with
disabilities—Fiction. 6. Samoa—Fiction.] I. Title.
    PZ7.B915126Bur 2007
    [Fic]—dc22
                                         2006029320

All Scripture quotations, unless otherwise indicated, are taken from The Holy Bible,
New International Version®, NIV®. Copyright © 1973, 1978, 1984, 2011 by Biblica, Inc.®
Used by permission. All rights reserved worldwide.

Cover design: Cindy Davis
Interior design: Christine Orejuela-Winkelman

Introduction

Most people think that the life of a traveling surfer is glorious. In many ways, it is; discovering cool places to surf and exploring new cultures is fun *and* exciting. But as anyone who spends a lot of time out on the road will tell you, sometimes being away from home and family can be a bummer ... especially if you like your home and family.

Because of this, Bethany's family often tries to plan their vacations around her surfing contests. As busy as they all are, the more remote the place is, the better. Spots well off the beaten path where there are no phones, computers, crowds, problems, or pollution are the best.

So, traveling to the beautiful island of Samoa in the South Seas for a surf camp sounded awesome.

But Bethany and her family soon discover that trouble can find you anywhere—even in the most remote of locations.

They will also discover that sometimes it's not the trouble—but how we react to it that's the true lesson ... and *gift*.

The Hamiltons are a typical family. Noah, the first son, is serious and business-minded. Tim, the second son, is a big goof-off who—he last time I saw him—had cut his hair into a mullet in order to be so uncool that he was cool. Tom and Cheri are caring, loving parents with more than a hint of old surf dog in them.

Bethany is pretty much like any other young teenager, except that she can surf really, really well. She has her ups and downs. She loves God and yet she still has room to learn and grow as a Christian.

Oh, and she has one arm.

But I'm sure you knew that already.

Keep in mind that I'm telling you a story—but not a story that is so far out that it couldn't have happened. In fact, some of it actually did happen. But like any storyteller worth his salt, I am not going to tell you which is which.

Enjoy!

Rick Bundschuh
Kauai, Hawaii

one

Bethany felt like she had stepped into another world—or *something* like that.

Still groggy from the plane trip from Australia, she blinked a couple of times and pulled her iPod headset down around her neck as she glanced around the busy little airport. Samoa didn't seem like the Treasure Island that her mom was so into talking about lately—but it did kind of feel like another world.

A world of giants.

Giants that wore knee-length wraparound skirts—or *lavalavas* as her mom called them. She watched the group of men as they passed her by with their suitcases and grinned to herself. *Bet no one would mistake them for girls!* She glanced at Noah as he fell into step beside her.

"*Big* people, huh?"

"I wouldn't want to play rugby against any of these guys," Noah admitted.

"You wouldn't last playing rugby against any of the *girls!*" Tim said, eyeing Noah's thin frame with a sly grin.

"I don't know—the girls are really pretty," Bethany laughed. "Might be worth the pain." Her attention was suddenly drawn to the group ahead of them. *Had to be surfers*, she thought, eyeing the three young guys with their sun-bleached hair and trademark broad shoulders. The youngest turned and said something to one of the older boys. Bethany guessed him to be close to her age. He had long wavy hair and his nose and cheeks were speckled from constant peeling. The bright red shirt he was wearing had the logo of a California surfboard company on it.

Surfers—I knew it! Bethany thought smugly.

"At least *I'm* not crazy enough to get a tattoo," Noah said as he shifted the board bag to his other shoulder. Bethany glanced back at him, momentarily confused.

"Tattoo?" She looked between her brothers and frowned. That's what she got for sleeping on the plane; she always missed the good stuff.

"*Samoan* tattoo," Tim nodded excitedly. "They're awesome; a lot of geometric design. Really tribal."

Bethany made a face. "Only thing I want on my skin is some sun."

"You're not getting anything tattooed, Tim," Bethany's dad said dryly from somewhere behind them as their mom laughed.

Tim grinned. "Or how about a *Maori* tattoo— you know, the big ones that cover your face?"

"Might be an improvement, Dad," Noah interjected.

"Don't give him any ideas," Bethany's mom said exasperatedly, and they all laughed as they headed for customs.

Other than the surfboards, the Hamiltons traveled light; each had a carry-on with shorts, bathing suits, T-shirts, and one set of "going to dinner clothes." They moved quickly through the line and into the night.

Outside, the warm humid air blew around Bethany, reminding her of home. She turned her face toward the star-spattered sky. Actually it *was* home, having her family with her. Even though it was almost midnight, she felt the excitement of being in a new place and couldn't help wondering what kind of waves she would catch this trip.

When she looked down again, she noticed a huge, dark-skinned man leaning against the van parked at the curb. He was wearing a flowered aloha shirt, a lavalava, and a pair of well-worn rubber slippers.

She saw his eyes take in their surfboard bags, and he began to wave wildly, charging over to grab the heavier of the loads.

"*Talafoa!* My name is Tagiilima," he said, extending a large palm to Tom, Bethany's dad. "You Hamiltons?"

Bethany's dad nodded, and Tagiilima vigorously shook his hand—along with the rest of his body.

Bethany's mom looked at her, and they both tried not to laugh.

"I am driver for the surf camp," Tagiilima announced with a wide smile to everyone as he began to relieve them of their boards and bags.

Then the Samoan caught site of Bethany.

He paused in his labors and stared at the tall, young blonde girl with a surfboard bag in her right hand and a knot in the T-shirt where her left arm should have been. A thoughtful look crossed his face as he took Bethany's board bag and secured it on the roof of the van with the others.

"I see you in magazine," he said softly. "Brave, strong girl."

Bethany smiled back shyly. It embarrassed her a little when people mentioned seeing her on TV or in magazines. She braced herself for the usual questions; "How big was the shark? Weren't you scared to surf again?" But the questions never came. Instead, the Samoan just smiled at her. There was something so honest and open about his face, she thought, almost like he was a kid in the body of a giant.

She liked him immediately.

The family piled into the van as Tagiilima finished cinching the surfboards on the roof rack. They were soon weaving their way down the amber-lit road that led from the airport to the town of Apia.

"Surf camp not far, but takes long time," Tagiilima announced, tuning to a Samoan radio station. "You can rest, sleep."

Bethany sat back and listened along to the strange mix of Western pop, Samoan, and Christian worship tunes as she tried to catch a glimpse of the dark island that raced past her window.

It was hard to see anything except for brief flashes here and there when a dim light shone from the porch or window of a building and, even then, the most she could make out was palm trees. Bethany sighed; it was hard to be patient when your whole body was itching to surf.

What was that her mom always liked to say about patience? She drew a blank and almost laughed out loud. *Guess I'm too wound up to remember!*

She glanced back at her family. Tim had commandeered the backseat and was sound asleep. Noah was wedged uncomfortably next to Bethany but had managed to doze off with the help of his ever-present iPod. Her dad nodded like a subway sleeper in the front seat while Tagiilima tapped his fingers to the beat from the scratchy van speakers.

Then she spotted her mom on the other side of Noah, impatiently straining her eyes toward the road as she tried to catch some passing scenery. Bethany couldn't help grinning.

An hour later, they were both leaning forward as the van passed the small sign that read Salani

Village and within minutes was crunching down a gravel road to the Salani Surf Camp.

A short, blond man who spoke with a kiwi, or New Zealand, accent appeared out of the dark as Tagiilima unloaded the luggage and surfboards. He wore a wrinkled and faded aloha shirt and a lavalava. Hiding shyly at his side was a small young girl with a tangled mop of curly light brown hair who was wearing an oversized T-shirt. Bethany guessed that she'd climbed out of bed to check out the new guests.

"Talafoa! Welcome, welcome! I'm Clint, your host. This is my daughter Maggie. Let me show you to your *fales.*"

Bethany glanced at her mom.

"Like a house," her mom, Cheri, whispered.

Clint guided the family to several large bungalows perched ten feet in the air.

"You can leave your boards underneath. They are perfectly safe. Hardly any Samoans surf, so they would be of no interest to a thief," Clint explained. Then he added with a crooked smile, "'Sides, if the village chief caught anyone stealing from a guest at this camp, he would smack the living daylights out of them."

"Nice," Bethany whispered to Tim, and he shot her a grin.

"The fales don't have bathrooms," Clint continued. "We have a large bathhouse with toilets and showers. All meals are served in our dining room.

I know you came in late, so we will serve breakfast until nine thirty. Oh, and I am afraid that there
will be no surfing tomorrow. It's Sunday, and local
village custom says we can't operate our boats or
encourage surfing on Sundays."

What?! Bethany glanced at her brothers who
appeared to be having as hard a time understand-
ing Clint's words as she was. Their parents had
taught them to honor God—that he came first
above everything else—but going surfing after
church was the norm for three kids that had grown
up in Hawaii. And surfing, after all, wasn't anything
like working.

"Actually, we were hoping to go to church in
the morning," Bethany's dad said, unfazed by
Clint's words as he stored his board underneath
one of the fales. "Is there one we can visit nearby?"

"Sure," Clint said with such a look of surprise
that it made Bethany wonder if it was the first time
he'd been asked that question by visiting surfers.
Or maybe it was the fact that none of them were
freaking out over the bomb he had just dropped on
them. *Bet those surfers I saw at the airport wouldn't
take the news so well*, she thought with a sniff.

She noticed Tagiilima smiling her way with that
big open grin of his and grinned back in spite of
herself.

Clint caught the exchange. "Ah, such a smile!
And she hasn't even heard the *good* news yet, has
she Maggie?"

Bethany was given her own fale to stay in, being the "unmarried girl" of their party. Samoan tradition, Clint told them.

Cool tradition, she thought with a huge grin as she threw her bag on one of the beds and glanced around her new little house. Even kind of Treasure Island-ish with its thatched roof, small desk, and two chairs. The floor was covered with a thick, woven mat and from the ceiling a rusty fan wobbled violently. It was perfect!

The screen door slapped behind her as she hurried out to the balcony. It was too dark to see anything, but she could hear the sound of the winds raking the palm branches. She closed her eyes and listened for the ocean, but for some reason the three surfers popped into her mind out of the blue. Then a funny thing happened. She suddenly felt urged to pray. Bethany took a deep breath, glanced up into the night sky, and prayed:

I don't know what this is all about, but I feel like I should say let this trip be about your plans—not mine, God.

All things work together for good for those who serve the Lord. She didn't know a lot about God's plans, but she was beginning to learn that much.

Bethany remembered a time when she had dodged God's urging and had almost missed having her pal Jenna in her life because of it. A wry smile tugged at the corner of her lips as she quickly added, *And please remind me that I prayed this—I've been known to forget everything when there's an awesome wave calling my name.*

Under the same Samoan sky Liam MacLeod studied the blanket of stars in the sky with little interest and definitely no intention of praying. He had made sure that their surfboard bags were safe before he settled down on the curb in front of the airport. But that was all he was going to do. Tucking his hands behind his head as he leaned against his backpack, he wondered how long it would take his cousins to straighten out the mess they'd gotten him into.

It was their fault, after all, he thought, allowing his anger to rush through him like a tidal wave. Getting angry seemed to be the only thing he was good at these days. Besides surfing, of course.

two

Bethany startled awake to her brother Tim banging on the door of the fale.

"Get up! Breakfast time! And Mom said to *hurry*!" he hollered, and she heard the heavy clomp of his feet as he crossed the deck and ran back down the stairs.

So much for privacy. She groaned, slipped into her shorts and T-shirt, and stumbled outside to the balcony.

In the light of morning, she could see in vivid color what had been muted in darkness last night. The surf camp sat on an outcropping of land with a small river flowing into the sea on one side and a deep saltwater lagoon on the other. She smiled as she finally spotted the ocean with its trail of white water breaking along a reef in the distance. *Man, I wish it was Monday!* She wanted to check out the waves so bad she could taste it.

The crunch of gravel and the sound of the camp van pulling into the courtyard broke into her thoughts. She turned to check out the new guests.

"No *way*," she whispered incredulously as three surfers slid out of the van—the same three she had seen at the airport and that had come to mind before she prayed. Too weird. Bethany watched Clint greet them and point the way to their fale, then she saw the youngest of the three stop dead in his tracks.

"Whaddya mean no surfing on Sunday?" he yelled, his voice breaking the stillness over the camp. Bethany cringed. *Okay, this guy's gonna be trouble.* Clint appeared to be explaining why they couldn't surf, when the young surfer made another comment she couldn't hear.

"Knock it off, Liam!" one of the older boys yelled. Liam gave them a look, abruptly grabbed his board and backpack from Tagiilima, and stomped off. Tagiilima stood stock still, as if stunned. The two older boys spoke with Clint for a few moments and then headed for their fale as well.

What a way to start the morning, Bethany thought, a weird sinking feeling creeping over her as she headed off toward the dining area to find her family. *Oh, man.* She frowned worriedly. *Everyone's been so excited about this trip. Just don't let him cause us any trouble, God.*

The dining area had a huge, thatched, palm-frond roof and a bar section where a TV set played nonstop surf movies. Above the bar the surf camp had items such as T-shirts, stickers, and postcards for sale. Smells from the kitchen greeted Bethany as she made a beeline to where her family was sitting, then stopped dead in her tracks.

There sitting at the table with Noah was a young brown-haired girl wearing dark blue shorts and a powder blue T-shirt. It was Malia, one of Bethany's best friends and surfing buddies.

Tim, who was standing at the buffet with a large piece of toast in his mouth, grinned at her.

"Surprise!" Cheri sang out from behind her, and Bethany glanced at her mom then back to her friend with a stunned look on her face.

"Malia?" Bethany sputtered as Malia grinned a big, Cheshire cat kind of grin.

"We thought we would surprise you," Cheri laughed. "Malia has been planning to join us since we first came up with the idea to surf Samoa."

Bethany was blown away. Having a good friend to share the adventures of a new place with was more than a wonderful surprise. It rocked! She gave her mom and dad a quick hug, then ran over and hugged Malia.

"Your mom wasn't freaked out about you traveling all this way alone?" Bethany asked as they sat down next to each other.

"Well, a little," Malia admitted with a grin. "At first she said she didn't think I could do it. But she finally caved when I told her that it was a nonstop flight and there would be someone from the surf camp to meet me when I got off the plane. I mean,

I'm *fourteen*—that's old enough to handle a little plane flight by myself!"

Bethany grinned. That's why she liked Malia so much. She had always been the kind of girl that threw herself into a challenge—especially if someone suggested that she might not succeed. *Two peas, one pod* was how her mom described them.

"I can't wait to show you around this place!"

"Let's eat first. I'm *starving!*" Malia laughed. "Then maybe we can do some surfing?"

"Uh, I guess no one told you—there's no surfing here on Sunday."

Malia gave Bethany a quit-pulling-my-leg stare.

"It's true! It's part of their culture, but maybe we can go exploring after church?"

"That's cool," Malia agreed easily, just happy to be with her friend. Bethany grinned.

"But right now we can explore some *food!*"

It was about twenty minutes later that Liam and his cousins strolled into the dining area— just as Bethany and Malia were leaving. The girls noticed Liam pause for a second, his eyes resting on the empty, knotted sleeve of Bethany's shirt for a long moment before he glanced over at Malia. He sneered, then brushed past them with an air of superiority ... and something else that Bethany couldn't quite put her finger on.

"Not the friendliest person, is he?" Malia said once they were out in the courtyard, crunching down the gravel walkway toward her fale.

"Not exactly," Bethany agreed slowly, still stinging from the way he had looked at her. She wasn't used to mean, spiteful looks like that, but she tried to shake it off, determined not to let it spoil her trip—or Malia's. He's someone else's problem, she told herself, not ours. She managed to smile then and hooked her arm in Malia's.

"Come on, let's get ready for church."

A few minutes later the family was assembled in the dining area wearing the only dressy clothes they had tucked away with them: simple skirts and tops for Bethany and Malia, a long floral print dress for her mom, and aloha shirts and shorts for the guys. Everyone's clothes had some creases from the trip, but Clint assured them the Samoans would be happy just to see them there.

It was a short trip down the gravel road into the small Salani village. Bethany, Malia, and her family got their first real glimpse of rural Samoan living: streets made of dirt and crushed coral where chickens and dogs roamed past brightly painted homes with tin roofs. Some of the houses were connected to an outside patio area with a thatched roof. As they walked, her mom told them that the patio areas were the fale of the house and the place where family members would eat, talk, and socialize with neighbors. Bethany noticed large concrete slabs sitting a foot or two off the ground in some of the yards. She glanced at Malia with a quizzical look.

"What are those things?" Bethany asked, turning to her mom.

"Your guess is as good as mine on that," Cheri said.

"They look like a tomb or flat gravestone," Bethany's dad said, squinting for a closer look. "See, some have flowers and words carved into them."

Malia nudged Bethany with a how-spooky-is-that look, and then they grinned at each other.

Suddenly a steady procession of children and adults began to emerge from the houses. The men were dressed in crisp white shirts, many with ties, and dark solid-colored lavalavas and sandals. Their hair was combed, and each had a fresh-scrubbed look.

The women and girls wore silky dresses of bright white. Some had hats as well.

"We are way underdressed," Malia whispered.

"Well, they don't seem to care, so maybe we shouldn't," Bethany whispered, noticing the warm, welcoming smiles as they followed the Samoans bound for the quaint little rock church on the corner.

As soon as they stepped inside, a large, smiling man in a tight white shirt called out in heavily accented English. "Talafoa! Welcome!" He shook her parents' hands and gestured to the line forming outside the chapel door. Something about him reminded Bethany of Tagiilima. She glanced around to see if she could spot her new friend, then felt Malia nudge her again.

She turned around to find about a hundred eyes staring at her as the children pointed at her empty sleeve and spoke rapidly to each other in their language. One of the little girls took off in a dead run out of the church.

"Super-stah," Malia whispered teasingly, and Bethany shook her head and grinned. The children's fascination with her missing arm didn't bother her at all. As a matter of fact, she felt nothing but warmth and acceptance from the Samoan people.

The truth was, she hadn't really felt like going to church—she would've preferred to be out exploring with Malia. But the peace that was settling over her after such a nasty encounter with that surfer made her think church wasn't such a bad idea after all.

Bethany and Malia took their seats with the rest of her family and looked around in awe at the beautifully carved wooden pillars scattered throughout the room. In the front of the church were a carved railing, a large table covered with an exotic-looking, lacy white tablecloth, and several big wooden pulpits covered with the same kind of lacy white cloth.

"How beautiful," Bethany whispered to Malia and her mom. Then she felt someone gently touch her shoulder.

It was the little dark-haired girl who had run out of the church. She was clearly embarrassed, and her hand shook a little as she held out the old copy of *People* magazine. It was dog-eared and creased. The magazine was turned to a page that showed a picture of a slightly younger Bethany and a large shark being held up by a backhoe.

The girl pointed at the picture, and then pointed at Bethany.

Bethany smiled and nodded yes.

The girl beamed in delight and quickly burst in a rapid-fire conversation with some younger children behind her.

"She must've recognized you and then ran home to find the magazine article," Malia said, sounding as touched as Bethany felt.

The children listened to the older girl and looked at Bethany with shy smiles.

"Big shark?" The girl said slowly. Bethany nodded and a thought suddenly came to her. She pointed toward the ceiling.

"Bigger God."

The girl looked at Bethany for a long moment, considering this. Tears suddenly filled her eyes, and she beamed a brilliant smile at Bethany before turning to walk away with her little pack of followers.

Without warning, a small Casio keyboard started up and the congregation rose to their feet. The keyboard player stopped playing but the congregation took up the song and kept it flowing in a rich texture of harmonies.

I've never heard singing so beautiful, Bethany thought and glanced to Malia and the rest of her family. They were clearly touched as well.

They tried to follow along but after a few feeble attempts at the Samoan language, they all were content to listen.

The Samoan church echoed with song after song of worship, each sung with gusto, the voices rising and falling like perfectly trained instruments.

After the singing, the pastor rose from a large velvet-covered chair that sat next to one of the pulpits. He was a large man with a coffee-bean color and a thick, heavyset body. By looking at him it was easy to imagine that in his youth he would have made a wonderful football lineman or rugby player—the sport favored in Samoa over American football.

He seemed to have a large heart as well.

Mounting the pulpit, he spoke to the congregation in Samoan and then, looking at the Hamilton family, he also spoke in accented but understandable English.

"And I want to say a welcome to our guests this morning," he said. "I will try to explain in English the things I am speaking about in our language."

The Hamiltons felt both honored and humbled by his generosity. They had merely intended on joining with other believers in a different land to see how they worshiped.

The pastor smiled and began his sermon, first in Samoan and then English. When he turned toward their group, Bethany felt as if he were preaching directly to her.

"We know that in all things God works together for the good of those who love him," he began in a deep, rich voice. Bethany's eyes widened in surprise. The same Scripture she had thought of when she was praying! She leaned forward as he continued. "'... who have been called according to his purpose.' Paul speaks this truth in the book of Romans. But what I would like you to ask yourself today and each day to come is, what is his purpose? I would like you to ask this even through the bad times. I say this because I have seen his great purpose revealed more in my struggles than in my triumphs."

Bethany sat back in her seat as the pastor continued his sermon, thinking about his words. How many times since the shark attack had people—including her own parents—told her that God had saved her for a reason? From the moment the pastor spoke those words, she felt like everything screamed into sharp focus around her. She glanced at her parents and Malia, all intent on the sermon. Then she glanced around the room. She felt as if God were trying to tell her something—but she wasn't sure where to look for the answer.

What is your purpose for my life, God? she silently asked.

The message came to a close, and the keyboard launched into the opening chords of a song that the congregation soared into with beauty.

The worship service ended, and Bethany's dad signaled for them to follow him out so they could acknowledge the kindness of the pastor.

At the door, the pastor greeted the Hamilton family and Malia warmly, introducing himself as Samuel.

"I would be honored to have you to my home for dinner while you are here in Salani," Pastor Samuel announced with a beaming smile. Bethany grinned as he shook her dad's hand with almost as much gusto as Tagiilima.

"We would be honored," Tom said earnestly.

"Wonderful! I will send someone to the camp to guide you to my house tomorrow evening!"

Bethany and Malia decided to lag behind and explore the village while the rest of the Hamilton crew headed back for camp. As they followed the little winding road through town, the girls quickly picked up a small following of children and a couple of scruffy dogs. The children eventually led them to a small stand where they could buy ice cream.

"Thanks for the tip on the ice cream!" Bethany called out to the kids as she and Malia chomped into the cool ice-cream bars. Bethany and Malia continued their journey through town without the children.

The girls could see inside many of the homes, and they marveled at the simple lifestyle of these people. It was apparent that they had little in the way of material possessions, but the homes were neat and clean, and their occupants happily greeted them as they walked by.

Bethany spotted one of Pastor Samuel's children and waved to the girl as she was going into her home.

"Must be where Pastor Samuel lives."

"Yeah," Malia took a bite of ice cream and leaned forward and squinted her eyes. "What do you think that is in the middle of his fale?"

Bethany peered through the holes in the decorative concrete blocks that made up the small wall around the fale. She could just make out a large woven mat in its center, decorated with red and pink feathers around the edges.

And, of course, it was hard not to miss the *body* under the mat.

All they could see were the large hands and feet sticking out ... and that one of the feet was missing a big toe. Whoever it was remained still as a stone. There was nobody else in sight.

"You think that's Pastor Samuel under there?" Bethany whispered.

"I don't know," Malia whispered back.

Bethany took another bite of ice cream, trying to decide what they should do—if anything. For a moment, she'd felt like she was either going to break into hysterical laughter or faint. Until she noticed the person was breathing. The mat rose and fell slightly each time the hidden man took a breath. She and Malia had seen a lot of unusual things, but nothing as strange as this.

Bethany looked at her friend. "The girls back home are never going to believe this, you know."

"Yeah," Malia nodded distractedly as she bit into her ice cream.

Bethany grinned and held up her cell phone. "Unless we have a picture!"

"I don't know." Malia frowned. "It seems kind of private."

"True," Bethany said, momentarily contrite, then she grinned mischievously. "How about just the missing big toe?"

"No!" Malia laughed. "You're as bad as Tim."

"Oh, really?" Bethany said, moving in on Malia with her cell phone. "Well then, how about a picture of you? I bet everyone would love to see that chocolate all over your face!"

Laughing and chasing each other, the girls finally wound their way back to the surf camp where they found Tim sitting at the bar, his mouth around a huge sandwich while he watched a surf movie. Clint looked up from the T-shirts he'd been folding.

"Hi, girls," he said with a smile, then he glanced sideways at Tim. "There's still some lunch to be had if you can get to it before Tim does."

Lunch was a salad bar with a do-it-yourself sandwich station. Bethany loaded up on salad while Malia made herself a giant sandwich that was only outdone by the monster Tim had created for himself.

"Have a nice walkabout?" Clint asked as they settled back at the bar.

"Yeah, it was fun for us to hang out together," Bethany said. "Except we saw something really weird."

"Way weird," Malia added.

"That being?"

"Some guy—or at least I think it was a guy—was on the ground with a big woven mat over his body on the fale at Pastor Samuel's house. But nobody was around."

"Ah," Clint said knowingly, "you just witnessed something really unique."

"What?" Bethany said, leaning forward.

"It's a repentance mat," Clint said, glancing between the two girls.

"What's that?" Malia asked.

"Well, here in Samoa if someone does something wrong, they haven't just hurt themselves or the person they wronged—they've hurt the whole village. When this happens, the person gets a chance to turn things around. If the person won't repent, he or she is kicked out of the village and can't come back. And because the villages are so interconnected, this person won't be taken in by any of them. He or she truly becomes a homeless person."

"What happens if he does say he's sorry?" Bethany asked, feeling a wave of guilt for making fun of something she had no idea about.

"If a person says he's sorry, he is expected to show it by going to the home of the chief or pastor to ask for the repentance mat," Clint continued. "The wrongdoer is put in the middle of the fale and the mat is spread over him. At that point, while he is covered up, anyone who has a grievance with that person can come into the fale and confront the person under the mat."

"What do you mean?" Malia said, exchanging a wide-eyed stare with Bethany.

"I mean they can yell at the person, give him a swift kick, or smack him with their hands ... without that person knowing who is doing it."

"Whoa!" Tim piped in and then turned back to his movie.

"Now, here's the clincher," Clint explained, leaning over the bar toward the girls. "The wrong-doer has to stay under that mat until the chief decides that he or she has shown repentance. It could be hours, or it could be *days*. But when the time comes and the chief finally lifts the repen-tance mat off the person, well, that's it! It's all over and done with. Nobody can give that person a hard time or hold a grudge. The person is forgiven, restored, and can return to the village like a new man or woman."

"That's so wild," Bethany said, taking a bite of salad.

"I can think of two people that need to go under that mat," Tim said suddenly, tearing his eyes away from the TV long enough to tease Bethany and Malia.

"Yeah? Well, you should be first in line," Bethany shot back with a grin. "Malia and I wouldn't have to worry after that; we'd be old and gray before the mat got lifted off of you!"

After lunch, Bethany and Malia headed back to their fale to prepare their surfboards for the days to come. Since traveling surfers remove the fins from their boards before putting them into the board bag, they needed to screw them back on, attach their leashes, and make sure there had been no damage to them during shipping.

The familiar crunch of gravel caused Bethany to look up from her board. "Tagiilima!" she yelled as she pulled Malia along to greet her new friend.

The Samoan stopped the van and leaned out the window as the girls approached. "Good morning, Miss Bethany and Miss Malia!" he said with genuine warmth.

"We went to church in Salani today," Bethany said. "It was really cool—I looked for you there—"

"I don't go today," Tagiilima said with a tight look around his eyes as he tried to smile.

He patted Bethany's hand. "I must go now. Drop van to Mr. Clint."

"I wonder what's wrong," Bethany said worriedly as she watched Tagiilima swing the van in next to the dining area and step out, his huge shoulders hunched over like he was carrying the world on them.

"He seemed okay to me," Malia shrugged. "Just kind of quiet."

"I don't know, Malia. His eyes looked so ... sad. And he is such a nice person." Bethany frowned. "I hope that Liam guy didn't give him any trouble after we left."

The girls glanced to the center of camp where Noah and Tim were engrossed in a game of volleyball with Liam's cousins Del and Hank. Tim had told them that the older boys' uncle offered to pay for half of their trip, if they brought Liam with them. They liked Liam but they were getting tired of babysitting him. And really tired of his outbursts.

Liam, by the way, was nowhere to be found.

three

Dawn bubbled up from behind the velvet green mountains as Bethany slid from her bed and stood over Malia's sleeping form. The air was still, hot, and muggy. The little wobbly fan had been working overtime to keep them cool all night long. Not that Malia seemed to notice, Bethany thought with a grin. She swatted her friend with a pillow.

"Wake up! Let's get something to eat and get going!"

Malia groaned in response and rolled over.

"Suit yourself," Bethany grinned again. "I'll just go surfing without you."

"Okay, okay," Malia said from under the pillow. "Give me a minute."

Bethany chuckled as she went out to the porch of the fale and started to stretch. She knew that taking the time to condition her muscles would help her stamina and looseness in the water.

As she stretched, she watched the sun spread across the sky like a watercolor, faint at first and then with a concentrated brilliance. A psalm she had read came to mind. She could only remember bits of it ... something like "God, my God how great you are! Beautifully, gloriously robed, dressed up in sunshine."

She paused in her stretching. Suddenly, she felt an overwhelming sense of God's majesty as awe for all he created washed over her. She drank in the towering mountains and lush green landscape. Sometimes she was amazed beyond words when she looked around at all he created.

"And yet, you choose to think of me," the words from a Third Day song rolled through her mind, and she smiled softly. *Thank you for blessing us with this awesome trip, God ... for all that you have done and are doing in our lives ...*

Her prayer was interrupted by the jarring sound of a rising argument coming from the porch of a neighboring fale. Bethany couldn't make out what they were saying, but she recognized Liam's voice—followed by Hank and Del's.

Bethany shook her head. How miserable it would be to have to stay with someone like that! Why couldn't the guy just enjoy his trip?

She turned at the slap of the screen door behind her and saw Malia standing there with a sleepy but startled look.

"What is going on over there?"

"I don't know," Bethany answered with a frown as she quickly finished her stretching and stood up.

She smiled wryly at her friend. "I just keep telling myself 'God works in all things.' "

Malia nodded thoughtfully. "Remember when we first met Jenna? We didn't know her story. I wasn't so sure how that was going to work out—-but God was."

"That's so weird that you said that; when we first got here, I thought of Jenna and everything that happened with her! I couldn't see how great she was because of how she acted with her mom."

Malia grinned. "Two peas ..."

"One pod." Bethany finished, with a grin of her own. "Now, hurry and stretch so we can go get some breakfast!"

Breakfast was laid out for them buffet style in the dining room. Bethany and Malia stood next to each other and surveyed their choices: eggs, sausage, bacon, fruit, bread, and yogurt.

"I can't make up my mind," Malia said. "Everything looks so good."

"Yeah," Bethany nodded. "Maybe we should just go with the fruit and yogurt this morning, so we don't bog down when we're surfing."

Tim came up behind the girls, his plate filled to the brim with eggs, bacon, and sausage.

"Hello, clogged arteries," he joked as he piled on the toast and butter. Bethany turned up her nose at him.

"I used to eat just like you, Tim," their dad said, looking up from the coffee cart. "If I tried to do that now I would weigh half a ton."

"Don't worry, Dad, I'll make up for you!" Tim said as everyone laughed.

The family gathered together at a table and, as was their habit, bowed their heads and blessed their food. When they lifted their heads, Bethany saw Liam and his cousins had entered the dining room just in time to view them praying. Liam rolled his eyes to his cousin as if to say, "Check out this goofy bunch."

Bethany felt Malia's hand on her arm and knew without Malia saying anything that she was telling her to remember their conversation back at the fale.

Even though Bethany wanted to say something, she was trying hard to keep her temper in check and remember the good that had come of what had been an uncomfortable situation with Jenna.

God, you are going to have to help me with this, she prayed silently.

"Boat leaves in ten minutes!" Clint said. The girls watched Liam and his cousins scramble for food as the Hamilton clan left to get their boards.

Within minutes, the boat dock was crowded with surfers and surfboards.

Liam strolled by the girls slowly, purposely eye-ing Malia's surfboard. Unlike the boards of many sponsored surfers, it was clean of all logos but that of its makers.

"How much did you have to pay for that?" he asked condescendingly. He acted as if Bethany wasn't there at all.

"I don't know," Malia shrugged. "It was a birth-day gift."

"I get mine free," Liam said. "As many as I want. If I break one, I just call my sponsor and get another."

Bethany noticed the word *sponsor* was empha-sized. She rolled her eyes.

"That's nice," Malia said, glancing at Bethany. "Bethany's sponsored too."

"Only because she was made famous by a shark," Liam said with a nasty smile.

Okay, that's it, Bethany thought, gritting her teeth. *I'm going to . . .*

"She was sponsored *before* that!" Malia shot back.

"Load 'em up," came the shout from the boat. They glanced over to see "Pod," with his iPod headphones glued to his ears, waving them for-ward. Soon, all the boards were loaded on the twenty-foot Zodiac boat. Captain Pod eased her off the berth and slowly turned up the engines as he guided the boat out across the shallow reef passage.

After safely navigating the sandbars and other obstacles, Pod gunned the engines as the boat headed into the channel.

Bethany and Malia made their way to the bow, hanging on tightly to the gunnels as they laughed with delight every time the boat bounced over a swell.

About a quarter of a mile off the shoreline, a crisp aquamarine wave could be seen rising up from the sea, zipping along and spitting spray from the hollow chamber as the wave ended.

Everyone on the boat hooted with excitement at the sight—everyone except for Liam.

Within minutes, Captain Pod was dropping anchor in a waveless reef pass as the surfers busily scratched one last coat of surf wax on the decks of their boards.

Bethany stood up first and tossed her surfboard into the crystal clear water. A moment later, she leaped in, headfirst. As she broke through the water, she saw bright rainbow-colored fish quickly dart out of her way.

The water was awesome. Bethany sucked in a huge mouthful and then squirted it out like a fountain. The ocean seemed to wash away her hurt and anger, and she felt the excitement of the day well up inside.

"Come on, Malia!" she called as she reached for her surfboard leash and slipped it around her left ankle.

Malia dove in, and soon the boat was surrounded by bodies and boards that splashed into the ocean. Bethany slid her board under her and started paddling for the waves looming up a hundred yards ahead.

As she approached the waves, she realized they were bigger than they appeared from the distance of the boat.

Awesome!

Bethany quickly stroked into the medium-sized wave and felt the bottom of the wave drop out as it moved over the shallow reef. Racing across the crest of the wave, she saw the section ahead of her was rearing up. She quickly tucked down into a ball and grabbed the rail of her board. The wave, hitting the coral studded reef, suddenly hurled over her head, placing her deep inside its pocket.

Everyone hooted excitedly as she rode the backside tube like a pro.

Bethany shot out of the barrel, stood tall on her board, and whooped as she flipped off the board. She laughed as she came out of the water and headed back for the lineup.

It felt a little crowded in the lineup, but she didn't mind. The California guys, including Liam, were decent surfers. Del and Hank displayed a bit of aggressiveness at first, paddling hard to get waves, but after a few rides they seemed to relax and share the fun with rest of the Hamiltons and Malia.

Hank and Del had known who she was when they first saw her at the camp. But watching her catch waves and leap to her feet with one arm absolutely amazed them.

"That chick is incredible," Del said to Hank.

"It's insane!" Hank replied. "Can you imagine trying to surf with one arm?"

As the morning wore on, Bethany found that Del and Hank were not only giving her waves but also offering low-key encouragement.

"Nice wave," one would comment to her after a ride. "You're ripping," another said.

But while Del and Hank found themselves admiring Bethany and warming to the Hamiltons, Liam, on the other hand, seemed to be hardening and getting more aggressive, especially toward the girls.

When a swell made an appearance and Bethany or Malia started to paddle for it, Liam would put himself in gear as well.

While he had talent, so did Bethany and Malia. And the thought of being outsurfed by two girls from Hawaii infuriated him.

Bethany and Malia usually ended up first to the takeoff spot and initially they tried to take turns with Liam. But they soon realized that he wanted *every* wave. The girls finally decided to take the waves they were in position for and let Liam deal with it on his own.

Liam did not deal very well. He started dropping in on the girls.

There are unwritten rules of etiquette in the sport of surfing.

One of the strictest rules is you don't drop in behind someone who has already caught the wave. Better known as cutting off or *burning*.

First one to catch it owns it.

While annoying at any surf spot, dropping in on a person at some surf spots has the potential to be very dangerous. Adding another surfer to the mix can cause the wave to swallow up the farthest surfer back if the wave is fast and hollow.

And the Samoan waves were fast and hollow.

Initially, Liam only dropped in on Malia or Bethany for a second and then pulled out of the wave, acting as if he didn't know they were there.

But later in the morning, as the other Hamiltons paddled back to the boat in order to catch a ride back to the camp, his intrusions became more and more obvious.

Bethany was starting to get fed up with his overt wave hogging. She began to mull over in her mind exactly what she wanted to say to Liam, or if she wanted to say anything to him, when the onshore winds begin to blow and all the surfers paddled back to the boat.

All the way over the reef, Bethany gave Liam a classic case of Hawaiian stink eye. Malia too simmered in silent exasperation.

Liam appeared not to mind the silent treatment.

After lunch, with the winds onshore, Bethany and Malia grabbed some snorkel gear and went off to explore the reefs that lined the shoreline. And to discuss what to do about Liam.

"I kinda want to talk to my brothers," Bethany said as they walked along the beach. "And then I kinda don't. I just can't believe we've come all this way to surf a spot and have something like this happen."

"God works in all things," Malia said with a wry smile. "At least I tried to tell myself that when we were out there. Maybe we should *say* something to him."

"I don't know if it would do any good. He would just say, 'Oh, sorry, I didn't see you had the wave, water was in my eyes' or something like that," Bethany said, frustrated.

"Maybe he got it out of his system today," Malia offered.

"I hope so," Bethany said. "'Cause if he does it again, I'm going to let him have it!"

"Ooo! You are so scary, Bethany!" said Malia with a smile. Bethany grinned back, and then they both raced each other into the water.

They gently floated over sharp coral, spiky sea urchins, and countless waving sea anemones. Small colorful fish darted back and forth underneath them and, from time to time, the girls spotted the sinister head of a moray eel. Picasso triggerfish trimmed along the edge of the reef showing off their brilliant abstract colors and looking for shells or coral to grind to sand with their tough teeth.

Suddenly, a grey reef shark swam up through a passage in the coral.

Malia let out a small squeal underwater and Bethany felt an electric shock go through her.

The shark was small. Too small to bother with human beings, but it was a reminder that they were visitors to this ocean world and that world contained not only beauty but also monstrous brutality.

Bethany had worked hard to get past the fear of sharks, but her reaction to this small reef shark reminded her that her dread of these creatures lay just under the surface.

Bethany pointed toward the shore, and Malia, who was also put off by the sight of a shark, nodded her head in agreement.

Minutes later, plopping down on the warm sand, Bethany glanced over at Malia. "You know, even those little sharks give me the creeps. I keep thinking that if there's a small one, there could be a big one real close."

"Yeah, I'm with you on that. And I don't like stingrays either," said Malia.

"How about jellyfish?" Bethany grinned, glad that Malia understood but didn't let her dwell.

"I hate jellyfish!"

"Have you ever been stung by a jellyfish?" asked Bethany.

"When I was younger," Malia said. "I didn't even see the thing. It just brushed against my arm when I was paddling, and then it burned like mad for hours!"

"I heard they have a real nasty kind in Australia," Bethany said. "It's so powerful it can kill you!"

"Disgusting things," said Malia.

"All this kind of stuff in the water. It makes you wonder why we surf."

"Yeah, we should be doing something safe—-like motorcycle racing."

"Or mountain climbing."

"Or extreme snowboarding in avalanche country."

"Brr! Too cold. I think I'll take my chances in the ocean," Bethany laughed.

By the time the girls got back to the camp, the winds had switched direction again. They scrambled for their boards and arrived at the dock the same time as Liam.

"Where's the boat driver? I want to go surfing!" Liam said, startling them both with his sudden burst of anger.

"His name is Pod," Malia said quietly as she glanced to Bethany. "I'll go see if I can find him."

Malia scooted toward the offices leaving Bethany alone on the dock with Liam.

Silence enveloped the pair for a minute or so and then Liam said, "So you're the one who lost her arm to a shark, huh?"

"Yeah ..." Bethany studied her board.

"Are you making lots and lots of money from going on television and being on billboards?"

"Yeah, I'm filthy rich," Bethany said, unable to hold her tongue any longer. "I'm down here to see if I would like to buy this surf camp, but now I think I will just buy the whole island instead."

"Ha, ha," sneered Liam.

Just then Malia returned followed by Pod, who was stuffing the last of a sandwich into his mouth.

"So, you want another go-out?" he said through stuffed cheeks.

"Yeah, the wind is offshore," Bethany noted with a small smile.

"The tide is a little low right now," Pod said. "It's surfable, but you need to be careful, especially on the takeoff."

A few minutes later the boat puttered out of the river and into the sea. Pod drove extra slow as the lower tide had made navigation over the reef passage far trickier. He dodged in and out of deep cuts in the coral while the nervous passengers kept an anxious eye on the water around the boat.

Eventually Pod found deep water and gunned the boat out to the break.

Even from the boat, Bethany could tell that the surf spot had changed since morning. The swell had picked up a foot or two of size, and the lower tide made the waves throw out sooner and thicker. A misstep anywhere down the line could mean a brutal wipeout.

"I brought the video camera," Pod said. "The sun is in a perfect position to get some great footage."

The three surfers hurled themselves into the ocean after their boards. Pod fished around in his ice chest for something cold to drink with one hand while digging out his video camera with the other.

With only the trio in the water, Bethany and Malia assumed that the surf session would be a far mellower event and that there would be plenty of waves to go around. But Liam, hearing that this session was to be videotaped, suddenly turned what surfers call *agro*.

With every wave, Liam tried to put himself into position. Sometimes he was successful; other times he paddled neck to neck with either Bethany or Malia.

"Gee whiz! This guy must think he is in a contest," Malia said to Bethany after Liam outraced her for a wave.

"He's trying to be a star for the camera," Bethany said with more than a hint of annoyance.

When a small lull occurred, and the three surfers found themselves sitting near each other, Bethany decided to use the opportunity to try and talk to Liam.

"Liam, there are only three of us out. Why don't we take turns?"

"'Cause I don't want to," Liam said. His jaw jutted outward as he looked for the next wave.

"It'll be more fun!" Bethany tried again.

"More fun for who? You two maybe," he shot back.

Suddenly, a large set appeared on the horizon. All three surfers saw it and started paddling frantically toward it.

Bethany gambled that the second or third wave would be larger than the first, so she kept paddling as Malia turned and stroked into the first of the giant swells.

Third wave, Bethany told herself as she paddled over the second swell.

As she had anticipated, the third wave was the largest in the set; and it jacked up and crested as Bethany spun her board around.

With one stroke, she entered the steep decline of the wave and launched to her feet. The speed of the drop surprised her a bit, but she planted the weight of her back foot and snapped the board up the face just in time to see the nose of another surfboard begin to enter the wave.

It was Liam, and he was about to drop in on Bethany at the most critical part of the wave.

The wave stood straight up on the reef and pitched out in a huge cylinder. Bethany found herself deep inside watching the white tip of Liam's board enlarge as he entered the wave ten feet ahead of where she rode.

The intrusion of the other surfer changed the mechanics of the wave. It suddenly sectioned off and collapsed on top of Bethany.

Bethany felt herself being rolled up the face of the breaking wave and then hurled down again. Somewhere in the foam and water was her surfboard. If she landed on it, she could be hurt. If the fins were up, she could be hurt badly.

The power of the wave swallowed Bethany up. She spun and rolled, keeping her hand and arm around her head in the event she collided with board or reef.

Opening her eyes underwater, Bethany saw only darkness. Then suddenly her foot touched the reef, and she withdrew it reflexively.

The pressure of the wave had driven her to the bottom of the ocean floor and was trying to hold her there.

Bethany reached up and grabbed the leash that held the surfboard to her leg. She climbed up the rope until her head broke through into a sea of foamy air. Then she looked at the nose of her board. It was cracked in two, the parts hanging by a thin skin of fiberglass.

Red-hot anger swelled up in her. As she paddled back to the boat, she wondered how in the world she was going to get through this trip God's way— and not hers.

As they headed to their fale, Bethany's mom met them on the path to remind them they were all going to have dinner at Pastor Samuel's.

"You have an hour to get ready, girls," Cheri said. Then noticing the two long faces, she couldn't help but laugh. "Come on! It'll be fun!"

Just great, Bethany thought. *Just what I need after the day I've had.* She glanced at Malia whose face seemed to mirror her thoughts.

On the hour, a young man in a lavalava and white shirt appeared at the surf camp. The Hamilton family and Malia were waiting in the dining room.

"You come for dinner at Pastor Samuel's?" he asked.

"Yes," replied Tom.

"I show you the way," he said with an eager smile.

It was still light out as the Hamiltons weaved their way back through the village. In the center of the village, the group came to a large cinder-block home—one all too familiar to Bethany and Malia. It was painted bright yellow and had lace curtains strung in the windows. Outside the home was a garage-size fale which sat several feet off the ground. The roof was thatched and the floor was concrete, covered with thick woven mats. There were no tables or chairs in sight.

Pastor Samuel, now wearing a colorful lava-lava and a white shirt with a red necktie sat cross-legged on the mat, surrounded by his sons.

"Talafoa!" he said, greeting the Hamiltons warmly.

"Talafoa!" Tom replied as the rest of the group watched the movements of their guide, trying to figure out what to do next. As soon as he dropped his sandals at the steps of the fale, they quickly did the same.

"Sit! Sit!" Pastor Samuel said, and they quickly plunked down on the mats around the pastor.

"Don't sit so that your feet are pointing at another person," Cheri whispered to the kids. "I read that it is considered rude to point your toes or the soles of your feet at someone."

Bethany stifled a giggle as she watched Malia glance at her feet with a worried expression. Bethany's mom had a way of picking out the strangest facts from travel brochures and books.

A few young women, dressed in beautifully printed long dresses, appeared at the door. Pastor Samuel spoke to them quickly, and then they left the fale and went into the house.

When they returned, they were carrying heaping plates of food: a giant red snapper, pork, yams, fruit, and poi. They set the dishes in front of Pastor Samuel who then offered up a prayer in both English and Samoan. After that, it was down to business.

Plates were passed out but no eating utensils. Bethany, Malia, and the rest of the Hamiltons played follow the leader. Using their fingers, they ripped chunks of fish off the plate and scooped in pork and rice in the same way. Pastor Samuel and his sons smiled their approval.

The food was awesome—and not that different from what Bethany would have eaten at a Hawaiian luau at home. Bethany hadn't realized how much she was eating until she glanced up to see Pastor Samuel nudge one of his sons and point to her with a happy grin.

At the end of the meal, the women appeared again bringing large mugs and a huge enamel coffee pot steaming with a scrumptious-smelling liquid. After passing the mugs around, the women filled each from the pitcher. Bethany peered into her mug. It smelled like hot chocolate — kind of looked like hot chocolate too.

Bethany glanced at Malia, lifted her mug and took a swig.

"Go ahead, Malia, it's really good," Bethany said, holding her mug out for more. Then she noticed people watching them from just outside the open-air fale.

They stood at polite distances or casually walked past, glancing at the family sitting cross-legged on the mats. More than once Bethany saw that the stares were directed at her.

"My people know of you, Bethany Hamilton," Pastor Samuel said, setting his mug down with a heavy thud. "My wife knows of you too. She said you were on TV. My people showed me a magazine with your story. They say you tell others about God. Could you tell me your story?"

Bethany cleared her throat and looked around. She'd never become totally comfortable speaking in front of people, but she said a quick, silent prayer and plunged forward, trusting like always that God would lead her through it. And he did.

The more she talked, the more she felt an inner push inside to keep going ... like this was something God wanted her to say.

She told about the morning it happened—how beautiful the sun and waves were—and how in an instant the fourteen-foot tiger shark had made everything go black. Then she told of how God had placed people at the beach to help her at just the right time—and how he had given her the courage to surf again.

"I didn't really expect all the attention that came after it happened," Bethany said finally. She glanced at Malia, and then she smiled a shy smile at Pastor Samuel. "I guess it's like your sermon; all things do work together for the good of those who love God."

Pastor Samuel sat back with a thoughtful look on his face.

"Yes, this is true," he said finally. "Now, I tell you a story about a man who also didn't expect God to use him in such a way. A man who came to our islands to die, but ended up teaching my people to live. He was called *Tusitala*, which in our language means 'Teller of Tales.' To others he was Robert Louis Stevenson."

The guy who wrote Treasure Island, Bethany thought as she glanced at her mom, and then at

Malia and the rest of her family. They were all leaning forward to hear the rest of the story.

"Tusitala was famous everywhere for his sto-
ries," Pastor Samuel continued. "But he was
famous among my people for his good heart ...
and his faith in God. With their bare hands, the
natives, chiefs, and all built a road for him from the
sea to his house. They called this road, *Ala Lota
Alofa*, the Road of the Loving Heart. My people
traveled this road many times to hear him speak
of God—to listen to the prayers he said to his
God—prayers he taught to them."

Bethany saw tears fill Pastor Samuel's eyes as
he paused for a moment. He smiled softly. "When
Tusitala died, the chiefs spread fine mats over him
and sat with his body in silence through the night.
Then, by torchlight, two hundred Samoans cleared
another road—one up the side of the mountain to
his grave. They carried his coffin on their shoulders
with songs to God. The chiefs forbade firearms
on the mountain after that so the birds could sing
over his grave." Pastor Samuel glanced at Bethany.
"Tusitala did not know he would touch so many.
But God did."

Pastor Samuel stood then, signaling that the
dinner was over. He shook hands with Bethany's
dad and brothers, and then surprised everyone by
the great bear hug he gave Bethany.

"Thank you, Pastor Samuel," Bethany said as
he finally released her. "For the dinner—and the
awesome story."

"And we know in all things God works for the good of those who love him." Pastor Samuel said with a wink.

"Well, Bethany, I guess you have a place to go if Mom and Dad ever kick you out," Tim chuckled as he and Noah headed to the dining room at the surf camp for a late-night snack.

Bethany stuck out her tongue at him, and Malia laughed.

"How can you two be hungry after all that food?" Cheri asked, exasperated.

"When aren't they hungry?" Tom laughed.

"Dessert!" Noah called out without turning around.

"Good night, Bethany and Malia," Cheri said with a chuckle as she kissed both girls. "Sleep tight."

"Night, Mom, Dad," Bethany said hugging her mom and then her dad.

"You might want to check under your fale in the morning," her dad whispered to her. "I think Tagiilima spent all evening fixing your board for you."

"That was a cool story, wasn't it?" Malia asked sleepily as they lay on their beds, watching the out-of-kilter fan go round and round.

"Yeah," Bethany said slowly. "I was just think-ing how mad I was about my board when we left for dinner. I was definitely not in the mood to go to Pastor Samuel's."

"What changed your mind?"

"I guess 'cause it was the right thing to do."

"And Tagiilima was working on your board the whole time ..."

"Yeah," Bethany glanced over and saw that Malia had drifted off to sleep. She turned and stared up at the ceiling again.

In the next fale over, Liam was wide awake as well. He had heard the Hamilton's banter when they came back from dinner—heard the love in Bethany's parents' voices when they told her good night.

Sleep tight, Bethany, he thought, feeding on a bitterness he didn't quite understand. But he welcomed it almost like a secret friend. It was better than being alone. *Don't let the bugs bite ...*

four

What time is it? Bethany bolted up in her bed and looked around. No Malia. She frowned, vaguely remembering Malia trying to wake her up earlier— and her telling Malia to go catch some waves for her.

Bethany grimaced. She'd had such a hard time falling asleep. The rusty fan wobbled as she tossed and turned, trying to sort out her feelings— wanting to have it out with Liam versus what she thought God wanted her to do. Was this trial in her life really going to be used for his glory—or was it just a silly problem between surfers? In the end, she again asked God to lead her—and that's when she finally fell asleep.

Bethany quickly got into her swimsuit and rubbed sunblock on her face and back. Then grabbing a towel from the drying rack, she bolted to the dining room.

Her mom and dad were still there, finishing up breakfast.

"We decided to let the youngsters take the first boat out," her dad laughed, then winked at her mom. Cheri cocked her head to one side and said, "We?"

"Okay, by the time *I* get there, Tim and Noah will be too worn out to make me look bad."

Bethany quickly wolfed down some fruit and yogurt, and then headed for the door.

"You don't have to rush," her mom called after her. "The second run doesn't leave for another twenty minutes!"

But Bethany was already heading for her fale to check on her surfboard.

There was a large dark spot in the center of the nose patch job. Upon closer inspection, the dark spot turned out to be a huge cockroach, stuck to the resin.

"Gross!" Bethany said out loud.

She got a small stick and began to pry the cockroach off the sticky trap.

"That wasn't there last night," Tagiilima's voice came from somewhere behind her. Bethany looked up from her work and saw the Samoan standing a short distance away with a troubled look on his face.

Bethany smiled at him. "It's no big deal—look, I almost have it off! Thank you so much for fixing my board."

Tagiilima drew closer to study the board and then nodded, apparently satisfied that the bug hadn't wrecked his handiwork.

"The boy say it would be good as new," he said with a shy smile.

"Boy?"

"Yes. American boy help me carry back to fale,"
Tagiilima said. Bethany's eyes grew wide as she
suddenly realized who the Samoan was talking
about. That cockroach stuck to her board was no
accident.

Tagiilima appeared to come to the same real-
ization as a grim look flashed across his face.

Fifteen minutes later, Bethany and her parents
were at the dock, loading their gear into the boat.
Pod was giving them the latest surf report straight
from the scene. The swell had come up; the waves
were pushing ten feet in height but the tide was a
little low. Everyone had to be very careful on the
takeoff or there would be some serious reef to
deal with.

Bethany pushed the troubling thoughts of Liam
to the back of her mind, allowing the wind and
the spray of the ocean to revive her as she looked
forward to joining Malia for a day of surfing.

five

Out at the break, Malia had joined the Hamilton brothers and Hank, Del, and Liam in the lineup. With the surf increasing in size and intensity, the nature of the session had turned from fun to heavy.

The waves on previous days, while powerful enough to break a board or give a good thumping wipeout, were by and large still in the playful category. Today the waves were challenging and potentially dangerous.

All of the surfers were being far more selective about the waves they chose. And being the youngest of the pack, Malia and Liam were getting fewer waves than the more experienced older surfers.

Malia didn't mind one bit. She stuck close to Tim and Noah; their constant encouragement helping to keep her fears at bay.

Liam, on the other hand, played the lone wolf. Truth was, he was frustrated—by his performance more than anything else. He aspired to be a big-wave surfer. In fact, he had often boasted of his big-wave skill. But now, in waves that would be rare at his California surf spot, he found himself hesitating and even freaking a little as he studied the hard-hitting ocean swells. He found himself cautiously selecting waves, making sure they didn't look as if they would close out all at once.

It is one thing to shred and carve a small manageable wave; it is another thing to try the same stunts in a cave of roaring water that can smack you into unconsciousness.

Liam kept out of the way of the main peak—the place where surfers launch themselves into the wave—and instead, drifted toward the shoulder where the drop would be less critical and punishing. When he glanced around for Malia, he saw that Malia had put herself squarely in the peak zone with Noah, Tim, Hank, and Del. The determined look on her face told him she was psyching herself to take off on the next set of waves.

It humiliated Liam to see her sitting there, but his fear kept him right where he was.

Pod guided the boat carefully around the protruding reef heads and into the deep water. "Wow!" Pod said, "The swell is really picking up. It's even bigger than when I dropped off the crew earlier."

The boat lifted high on the incoming swells and dropped with a lurch.

"Whoa!" Bethany's dad said with a laugh as the boat slapped the bottom of the wave.

Bethany, riding on the bow, stared in awe as the surf spot that yesterday had been like a day at the carnival now heaved and hurled with deadly power.

The boat stopped and everyone started preparing their gear—everyone except Bethany's mom. Cheri was no longer a fan of the mean, rough-and-tumble waves that she saw.

Pod scrambled to find a second anchor and heaved it overboard.

Bethany stood on the bow for a moment and then tossed her board into the water, following after it headfirst. Paddling toward the break, she saw the dark hint of an oncoming set of waves on the horizon.

The surfers in the lineup saw it too, and they scrambled out to sea.

The massive waves were coming at them in perfect rhythm, one after another. Noah went first, dropping down the huge wall of water and then pulling off the bottom, putting himself high on the wave for maximum speed.

Those still paddling out hooted in approval.

Del and Hank caught the next two, both men charging down the double overhead face and blasting toward the channel.

Liam held out on the sets. But then he saw a wave that he knew he could catch from his perch on the shoulder. He spotted a small, lithe figure paddling hard in the peak of the wave.

It was Malia.

Why Liam did it, he was never sure. Maybe it was because he was frustrated that he wasn't catching waves, maybe it was because he was scared that an even bigger bomber would be marching in behind these waves to clean him up. Maybe his ego couldn't stand the thought of a mere girl taking off at the peak while he hung out on the shoulder.

All these things may have rolled through his mind as he paddled for the wave that Malia was now starting to catch.

As Malia dropped down the face of the monster, the water began to drain off the reef, getting sucked back up the wave. A huge growling sound of wind, wave, and exploding water surrounded her. She set her stance hard and raced out in the flat water before turning hard up the face.

Suddenly she saw, farther down the wave, Liam taking his last paddle. He looked directly at her as she pulled off the bottom of the wave and cranked the board up the face where she could get the speed to race down the wave before it collapsed on her.

Liam, with impassive eyes, took in Malia's critical situation for a moment, and then stood to his feet and dropped into the wave.

"Nooo!" Malia cried out—too late.

Liam had made up his mind. He would take this wave.

It was the ultimate burn.

Malia knew that Liam's move into the wave would cause it to break prematurely, increasing the chance of her being picked off by the incredible power of these waves.

She also knew that she had no other choice but to try to outrun the lip of the wave and catch up with Liam.

As Malia pulled up high on the face of the wave she saw that the track of Liam's board was causing the whole section of wave in front of her to collapse.

What happened next took only seconds, but for Malia it was like a slow-motion train wreck.

Crouching low, hoping to slip under the lip, Malia drove hard, but she was too late. The thick upper portion of the wave drove into the light girl like a jackhammer, slamming her off of her board and pitching her into momentary weightlessness.

Before she impacted the water, she saw the terrifying sight of water draining off the reef. She knew she would have little, if any, cushion of water to land on.

Liam had not only burned her. He had doomed her.

She buried her head in her arms and tried to flatten her body so as not to pile drive into the shallow water. Somewhere behind her, in a mass of white and green turbulence, her board followed.

Malia slammed into the shallow water followed within microseconds by the whole force of the wave.

Hands held tightly over her head, she felt herself bump and roll over the reef in an uncontrollable cartwheel.

Bethany, paddling out, saw the whole thing.

She saw Malia drop into the critical wave. She saw Liam knowingly stare at her friend and then drop in on her.

She saw Malia make a valiant but hopeless run at the closing out section.

She saw the water drain off the razor sharp reef right at the impact point. And she saw the brutal wipeout.

Her stomach turned.

The impact knocked the wind out of Malia. Thoughts ripped through her mind; she was a rag doll in the mouth of a big dog wave—shaken, twisted, and turned.

The white-hot sensation of pain came suddenly to her knee as it collided with a coral head, and Malia finally opened her eyes.

Around her was darkness, but above her was light. She struggled toward it.

Bethany quickly paddled toward the inside of the break, where she knew the wave would hurl Malia.

Mercifully, the wave her friend caught was the last of the set. A short lull followed. Otherwise Malia may have been held under again and again as each wave expended its energy on her. Bethany spotted two pieces of surfboard on the surface of the water. She knew that one of them would have Malia attached to the other end. She began to paddle frantically as she spotted Malia bob to the surface.

A tint of red blood rose up around them as she edged her board closer to the spot where Malia was struggling to keep her head above water.

Just then Cheri paddled up next to Bethany. "Let me do it."

It made sense for Cheri to be the one to snatch Malia; she had the long board and the use of both arms.

"Go get her, Mom," Bethany said.

Cheri eased her board next to Malia and scooped her up in front of her.

As weak as she was, Malia helped Cheri to paddle out of the danger zone.

Bethany stroked alongside Malia, remembering that when she found herself hurt after the shark attack, their friend Alana paddled beside her as she was towed to safety.

On Malia's arms and legs Bethany could see tracks of blood trickling down from unseen wounds. The thought of sharks came to mind. But she forced the idea out of her head and paddled hard toward the boat.

Pod had already moved the boat in closer to the rescue, knowing the other surfers would catch up. He quickly helped get Malia aboard, and Bethany held her hand as Cheri began to check out Malia from head to toe. Malia winced and moaned; she had numerous gashes and razorlike slices all over her body. Behind some of those gashes, bruises were already forming. On her right knee, a steady stream of blood poured down her leg.

Bethany didn't need to see the expression on her mom's face to know the wound was serious. The coral had sliced through the flesh and gone all the way to the bone, clipping several small veins. There was a nasty three-inch gash alongside her kneecap.

"We've got to take her to the hospital!" said Cheri.

Pod gave a brief nod, seeing the extent of her injuries.

One by one the other surfers climbed aboard the boat, each one stumbling with the boat's pitching as they tried to see what was going on.

"Oh no! The little charger got hurt!" Hank exclaimed.

"Yikes! Oww!" Tim said, wincing when he saw how cut up Malia was. Then he added, "We'll get you patched up. Don't worry, girl."

"What happened?" Bethany's dad asked as he climbed aboard.

"Bad wipeout," was all Bethany's mom said. Bethany remained quiet as she helped her mom wrap the bleeding knee in a towel. Then she looked up to see Liam climbing aboard.

He slinked past them to the opposite end of the boat without saying a word.

Pod gunned the boat and raced toward the camp.

At the dock, Noah and Tom picked up Malia and carried her to the dining room. Clint came out of the office with a huge first-aid kit and proceeded to pour hydrogen peroxide on every cut. The liquid bubbled as it hit each open wound.

"Staph infection is the worry around here," he said to no one in particular. "The cut could be minor, but if it gets infected you have a real night-mare on your hands."

The whole camp, except for Liam, who had slinked off to his fale, gathered around Malia as Clint went to work.

Using butterfly bandages, Clint closed the slice on Malia's knee. "This one is gonna need stitches." He cleaned off Malia's foot; a few little black dots circled her heel where she had clipped a needle-like sea urchin.

"The only real hospital is in Apia," Clint explained as he closed up the kit. "It's called the Tupua Tamasese Meaole Hospital. We should take her there for stitches and to get her checked out. Tagiilima knows where it is. He's got the van ready to go."

"I'll go with her," Bethany's mom and dad said at the same time.

"Me too," Bethany said and then folded her arms when she saw her parents' hesitation. "She's *my* friend."

"Okay," Cheri said. "Hurry and get some clothes on—get some for Malia too."

Bethany ran to the fale, hurriedly changed clothes, and grabbed some fresh clothes for Malia. By the time she got back to the dining room, Malia was already in the van.

"How ya doing?" she asked softly as she slid in next to her friend.

"I hurt all over," Malia said, a slight tear, her first, appearing in the corner of her eye.

"I saw what happened," Bethany said, leaning in close. "That creep Liam burned you!"

"I know," Malia said. "He looked right at me and then dropped in." After a pause, she said, "I don't know why he did that; he knew how shallow it was. It was as if he was trying to hurt me."

"Well, I don't care why he did it," Bethany said. "When my brothers find out what happened, they will make sure he isn't surfing anymore."

"I don't think *I* will be surfing for a while."

"Aw, you'll be back real fast," Bethany said, even though she wasn't so sure that was the truth. She bit her lip and glanced up to see Tagiilima give her an encouraging smile from the rearview mirror.

Her parents quickly piled into the van and Tagiilima threw it into gear, spitting gravel from the tires as he headed toward the hospital.

En route, the family discussed what could be done about Liam. His actions in the water weren't considered illegal, but he had definitely crossed the line.

Bethany wanted to sic her brothers on him. In her mind's eye, she could picture Liam giving Tim lip service—and then Tim knocking him through the wall. Bethany smiled wryly. Not that Tim was exactly like that—but she always liked to imagine her brothers giving bad guys the licking they deserved.

Her dad thought a stiff lecture would be good.

Her mom wanted Clint to boot him out of the surf camp, but then her dad pointed out that Del and Hank would have to go too.

Everyone agreed that it wouldn't be right to punish two innocent guys for the stupidity of their younger cousin.

As they approached Apia, Tagiilima spoke. "The yellow-haired boy who did this to Miss Malia is bad?"

"A complete jerk," Bethany said, letting her temper get the better of her.

"If he were in my village he would have to go under the repentance mat," Tagiilima said, watching her in his rearview mirror.

"I'd like to get him under a mat," Bethany said dryly. "I'd kick the daylights out of him."

Tagiilima laughed.

"I understand, I understand," he said and then was quiet again.

A few minutes later they pulled up to the entrance of the hospital. Bethany's parents quickly helped Malia from the van.

"I will be waiting for you in the parking lot," Tagiilima instructed.

"You don't have to stay in the van by yourself," Bethany said with a frown.

"I pray," Tagiilima said simply.

Bethany paused with her hand on the door. She looked at Tagiilima again and smiled. She had a feeling there was a lot more to this quiet and respectful driver than she imagined. Tagiilima smiled back as she shut the door.

six

"How did this happen?"

"Surfing accident," Malia said, wincing.

The doctor raised his eyebrows and put on his eyeglasses. "We don't get many of those in here, and you are certainly the youngest—and the only girl I've ever treated for a surfing accident."

Bethany saw Malia smile weakly at the doctor before she winced again. Her body was covered with numerous lacerations, and the bandage on her knee was red with blood. Just before the doctor had come, Malia had confided in her that she felt as if she'd been run over by a bus. Bethany noticed the hundreds of little slashes in her bathing suit and rash guard and gritted her teeth.

"The first thing we need to do is to suture up that cut on your knee," the doctor said as he explored Malia for other cuts. As his hand passed over her left side, Malia winced.

"And I want to get you X-rayed as well. You seem a little tender around your ribs, and I want to make sure nothing is broken."

Bethany bit her bottom lip—hard.

She saw him fill the needle with fluid from a bottle and knew that he was going to numb Malia's knee before scrubbing out the wound and sewing it up. She couldn't bear to watch.

"I'll be right back," Bethany said, quickly slipping down the hall to the waiting room while her mom stayed by Malia's side.

"This is so horrible," she said, slumping down in the seat next to her dad. "Malia comes all this way to surf—then because of some jerk, she's out of the water for the rest of the trip."

"I agree," her dad said. "But I'm just glad she wasn't hurt worse. People have died from being dragged over ragged reefs like that."

"I know ..."

It seemed like forever until her mom and Malia appeared. Malia had a fresh bandage on her knee and was dressed in the clothes that Bethany had brought for her. Bethany hugged her tight as her mom went to call Malia's parents.

"The X-rays showed no broken bones," said Malia.

"Let's see your stitches," Bethany said, putting on her best face as Malia carefully pulled the bandage back to reveal her tightly sutured wound.

Bethany counted them. "You have ten!"

Malia grinned. "Yeah, I've never had stitches before."

"Really? I'm an old pro at getting them."

"Even before the attack," her dad chimed in. "Bethany was always coming home bleeding from something. I thought our health insurance was going to cancel us if we showed up at the emergency room one more time."

"It's the price of adventure," Bethany said, glad to see Malia smiling again.

"Well, I think I've had enough adventure for one day," said Malia.

"Let's go find Tagiilima and get something to eat!" Bethany said. "I'm starving—how about you, Malia?"

"How about it, Malia? Are you hungry?" Bethany's dad asked.

"The only part of me that doesn't hurt is my stomach," Malia said with a grin. "So I might as well fill it!"

"Thatta girl," Bethany said, and they all laughed.

The family found the camp van parked in the lot under the shade of a tree. Tagiilima was in the front seat, his head bowed.

"Is he sleeping?" Bethany asked.

As they approached the van, they could see that Tagiilima wasn't asleep at all. His eyes were closed but his lips were moving, as if he were having a private conversation with someone.

Hearing the footsteps of the group approach, he opened his eyes and jumped out of the van excitedly.

"So glad to see you are okay, Miss Malia," he said. "I have been asking my Father to help you not be hurt badly."

"You mean you have been sitting in the car praying this whole time?" Bethany asked, glancing to her parents.

"Yes, it is good!" Tagiilima said kindly. "I ask God to help Miss Malia. I ask God to help the boy too." A thoughtful look crossed Tagiilima's face. "Something makes his heart mad."

Bethany paused with her hand on the door and felt shame trickle through her. For the first time since Malia's accident, she was reminded of her own prayers.

Her good friend had been hurt, and the whole time she was in the hospital all she could think about was getting revenge on Liam. Talking to God hadn't been on her mind at all.

Bethany studied Tagiilima's face, and then smiled at this man who had spent the last few hours in prayer for all of them. *Help me to be more like him, God*, Bethany prayed.

Tagiilima smiled back as she shut the door.

When the van finally pulled onto the gravel driveway of the surf camp, Noah, Tim, Clint, Pod, Del, Hank, and a number of kitchen workers came out to greet them.

All were very pleased that Malia was up, moving, and in good spirits—and even laughed when they heard she ate more ice cream than Bethany *and* Tagiilima. They had feared that she might have been hurt much worse.

The kitchen staff brought out steaming mugs of hot chocolate, and the whole camp settled into the dining room to celebrate Malia's return.

All except for Liam.

Liam's cousins had pulled him aside shortly after Malia had been rushed to the hospital and given him a stern lecture. Both of them vowed that they would never take him along on any surf trip in the future. Then they demanded that he apologize to everyone and told him that he would have to pay for Malia's medical bills.

Liam was feeling sorry for himself. *No telling what Tim or Noah will do to me*, he thought grimly. And he couldn't count on his cousins to help him—not anymore.

Liam quickly packed his clothes and what money he had in a daypack and quietly left the surf camp.

Originally, his plan was to hitchhike into Apia. There he would find a hotel for the night and call his father and have him get him a plane ticket home. As he hiked down the narrow road out of the village, the plan seemed to unravel in his mind.

The road was desolate. A few motor scooters buzzed past but not much else. One or two cars came from the other direction, probably people who worked in Apia heading home for the evening. And it was way too far to walk.

Liam glanced around. He was alone. He was
in a strange country with a strange language—
and everybody hated him. Well, *he* hated Samoa,
he hated his cousins, he hated the surf camp. He
hated the Hamilton family—especially Bethany
and Malia for making his life miserable.

Liam frowned, feeling the guilt slowly burn
through him—in spite of his efforts to blame
everyone else.

Deep down, he knew he had done the wrong
thing by dropping in on Bethany and, especially,
Malia. He knew he had been mean without any real
reason, but his pride wouldn't allow him to admit it.

Instead, he continued to trudge down the dark
road alone.

After the hot cocoa, Bethany and Malia went
back to their fale and got ready for bed. Bethany
fluffed up Malia's pillow, made sure the lopsided
fan was going full blast, and then grabbed her
Bible and sank down into her own bed.

In a strange sort of way, finding Tagiilima
praying—at the same time she'd been plotting
revenge—had been a turning point for her.

Bethany cracked open her teen Bible to the
book of Matthew and began to read:

> Jesus stepped into a boat, crossed
> over and came to his own town. Some
> men brought to him a paralytic, lying
> on a mat. When Jesus saw their faith,

he said to the paralytic, "Take heart, son; your sins are forgiven."

At this, some of the teachers of the law said to themselves, "This fellow is blaspheming!"

Knowing their thoughts, Jesus said, "Why do you entertain evil thoughts in your hearts? Which is easier: to say, 'Your sins are forgiven,' or to say, 'Get up and walk'? But so that you may know that the Son of Man has author-ity on earth to forgive sins ..." Then he said to the paralytic, "Get up, take your mat and go home." And the man got up and went home. When the crowd saw this, they were filled with awe; and they praised God, who had given such authority to men.

Take your mat and go home ...

Bethany closed her Bible. How cool was it that she would find Scripture like that after learning about the repentance mat?! Even better was what Jesus had said to the crippled man: "Your sins are forgiven. Take your mat and go home." He didn't wait to consult anyone that the man might have wronged. He didn't yell at him or make him feel bad, he just forgave the man.

Bethany let her mind wander as she tried to imagine what in the world the crippled man could have done as far as sin.

Did he drag himself over and steal the coins from his fellow beggar? Did he swear at someone who stepped over him or on him? Did he end up paralyzed because someone caught him robbing their home and beat him up?

Too bad there aren't more details about these kinds of things in the Bible, Bethany thought. Then another thought occurred to her: *Maybe the details of the sin aren't as important as people knowing that Jesus can and will forgive anyone that comes to him.*

Whatever the wrongdoings the crippled guy had done, when Jesus forgave him it was over. Done. He was free. And then as a bonus, he was healed of his physical handicap.

Lying in bed, with her open Bible draped across her body, Bethany let go of her desire to extract revenge from Liam. She let go of her anger and bitterness.

"Malia, you still awake?" Bethany asked quietly.

"Yeah?"

"How do you feel about Liam?"

"Well, he's not exactly my favorite person right now, if that's what you're asking," came the muffled reply.

Bethany tried not to grin.

"I mean, do you want revenge? Do you want to see him suffer for what he did to you?"

"Maybe I should ..." Malia said slowly. "But I prayed about it, and even though I don't really like

82

him for what he did … I don't know … I kinda feel sorry for him. He seems so, so mixed up and hostile, kinda like he is angry at the whole world."

"Something makes his heart mad," Bethany said softly.

"What?"

"Tagiilima said it earlier. He said he was praying for Liam because something made his heart mad."

"It makes sense," Malia said. "People are usually mad for a reason."

"You and Tagiilima have such a cool way of looking at things," said Bethany. "And then there's me, wanting to chop him into hamburger."

"Yeah, but you don't feel like that anymore, right?"

"No—not after I prayed," Bethany admitted.

"Then we're not so different."

Bethany laughed. "Two peas?"

"One pod," Malia finished, groggily. "Now go to bed. I still feel like a bus ran over me."

seven

It was a moonless night, and the stars, while brilliant, could not penetrate the canopy of trees under which Liam walked. So dark. He couldn't remember ever being somewhere this dark.

Strange noises were everywhere. He could hear the grunts of wild boar in the distant bush and the croaking of toads in the watery ditches nearby. Unseen bugs buzzed in the trees. He felt the breeze of something shoot by his face and swatted at the air frantically.

It seemed crazy to go on. He had no food or water with him. And no cars had passed for a long, long time. Part of him wanted to give in and go back to the surf camp—but another part of him couldn't allow it. That would mean he would have to admit to everyone how wrong he had been.

"Why are you so mad, Liam?" his father's voice whispered through his mind, reminding him of the conversation they had just before he had boarded the plane. Liam glanced over his shoulder, almost wishing that his father was behind him. But he wasn't.

Why are you so mad, Liam?

Not knowing what else to do, he finally sat down on a large gravestone he spotted at the edge of someone's property. Then he pulled his legs up underneath him and quietly began to cry.

Back at the surf camp, Del and Hank had just returned to their fale after watching a movie with the Hamilton brothers when they both noticed Liam's empty bed.

At first they gave it little thought, figuring Liam was out messing around somewhere as usual. But as the night wore on, they started to worry. Finally, worry gave way to action, and they set out to scour the camp for Liam.

Bethany and Malia were sound asleep when Tim pounded on their door. Bethany struggled up and opened the door to find her brother staring back at her, hair all askew, eyes wide with worry. She suddenly felt wide awake and alert.

"What's wrong?"

"Have you seen Liam?"

"Um, no," Bethany frowned. "Why?"

"We can't find him," Tim said. "And we've looked everywhere. Del and Hank are starting to freak out."

"I'll help you look," Bethany said, reaching for her clothes.

"Me too!"

"No, Malia!" Bethany said, shrugging her shirt on. "You don't need to be hobbling around in the

dark. You'll trip and fall in a hole or something—-
then I'll have two people to worry about. Just hang
out here. I'll let you know what's up."

Out of her dresser drawer, Bethany pulled a
small flashlight and stuck it in the pocket of her
shorts.

"God works in all things, huh?" Malia said, and
Bethany paused at the door.

"What do you mean by that?"

"You said you would have two people to worry
about," Malia said. One being me—that means
the other person would have to be Liam."

With that parting comment, Bethany shut the
door and disappeared into the dark.

The search for Liam had grown to involve
almost everyone at the camp. Bethany's parents
searched down by the docks with Clint while the
boys searched the vacant fales. Bethany spotted
Tagiilima sliding behind the wheel of the van and
ran over to him just as he was starting the engine.

"Can I come too?"

"Yes, Miss Bethany," Tagiilima said with a worried look on his face. "You come look, help find!"

"Can we pray before we go?" Bethany asked
a little tentatively and then smiled when Tagiilima
bobbed his head excitedly.

"Yes, Miss Bethany, we pray!"

Bethany grabbed his hand and said a short
prayer asking God to lead them in the way they
should search and to help them find Liam safe.

"Amen," they both said together, and Bethany quickly slid into the van next to Tagiilima.

Crunching the tires over the crushed coral and gravel driveway, Tagiilima steered the van down the small road that served as the main highway around the island.

"We see if he is walking first," the Samoan suggested. Bethany pulled the small flashlight out of her pocket and turned it on. The beam was narrow but bright.

"Thank goodness for new batteries," she said, sweeping the light back and forth as the Samoan drove slowly down the road.

Please God, help us find him, she silently prayed. *I do believe all things work together for your good. Let something good come of this.*

Several miles from the camp, Bethany's sweeping light ricocheted off something reflective. Hope surged though her body.

She swept her light back toward the object and held it firm.

The light was bouncing off the reflective strip of a daypack.

It was then that she saw the huddled figure of Liam.

"He's over there!" Bethany said excitedly as Tagiilima quickly swung the van around and drove up next to where Liam was sitting.

"Liam! Everyone is looking for you!" Bethany said gently as she stepped from the van.

Liam didn't move or even lift his head.

"They are worried about you. We were *all* worried about you."

The boy slowly lifted his head. His long blond hair was swept back by a sudden gust of wind and Bethany saw the tears on his cheeks.

"I screwed up," Liam said softly. "Screwed up big time."

"I know," Bethany said, easing closer. "But we all screw up every once in a while. Come get in the car. Please."

Liam slowly unfolded himself and, like a man going to the gallows, he crawled into the backseat without looking at either one of them.

"Pick up your mat and go home." Bethany whispered softly—not realizing she had even spoke the words out loud until she saw Liam and Tagiilima looking at her like she might be a little crazy.

"What?" Liam sniffed.

"It's something I read earlier—from my Bible," Bethany felt her cheeks flush, but she took a deep breath, whispered her silent prayer for help, and went on. "It was about this crippled guy whose friends had so much faith that Jesus could help him, they took him to where Jesus was. Before the guy said a word, Jesus told him his sins were forgiven ... and to pick up his mat and go home."

"I thought you said he was crippled," Liam said softly, and Bethany was surprised to see Tagiilima lean forward, as if he was anticipating the outcome of the story as much or more than Liam.

"That's the cool thing; Jesus didn't just forgive him of his sins—he healed him too. It was like, because he believed, he was forgiven and made whole. *Everything* was new. That's how it is with God; you don't have to feel guilty ... or pay."

"Pick up your mat and go home," Tagiilima said softly. When Bethany turned and smiled at him, she was surprised to see tears in the big Samoan's eyes. "Like the repentance mat."

Bethany nodded excitedly and turned to Liam and explained the cool similarity between the custom of the Samoans with the repentance mat and the story about Jesus healing and forgiving the crippled man.

"I feel like I've been under the repentance mat since I left camp," Liam said quietly.

"But you don't have to stay there," Bethany said. "We've all done things to hurt others. We've all put ourselves at the center of the universe. We've all wished we could be number one. So we all deserve to be put under the repentance mat.

"But the wonderful thing, the thing that makes it a different story, is that God comes to us and lifts off the mat. By dying on the cross, Jesus took the punishment we deserve. Because of him, we are forgiven and free."

"I'm not sure about all this religious stuff," said Liam.

"I'm not talking about religion," Bethany said with a smile. "I'm talking about having a relationship with God. Actually getting to know him!"

"How do you do that?" asked Liam.

"It's simple! Just ask forgiveness and put your trust in him. He took the mat off you and put it on himself!"

"We can pray!" Tagiilima said, suddenly beaming with that wonderful smile of his.

"Yes! Please, Tagiilima," Bethany said. "You lead us."

Tagiilima began to pray out loud, his imperfect English mixing with Samoan words.

"Please help me," Liam whispered brokenly, surprising both Bethany and Tagiilima as he began to cry. "I've been so mad since my mom died ..."

What happened next, Bethany knew she would remember for the rest of her life. She felt tears fill her own eyes as she watched the huge Samoan move to the back of the van and take Liam gently in his arms as he too began to cry, sharing in Liam's grief—as well as his new life.

By the time Tagiilima, Bethany, and Liam pulled the camp van into its parking slot, the mood at camp was frantic. Tim ran toward the van as Bethany leaned out and called, "We found him; he's okay!"

A timid and fearful Liam exited the van fully expecting the rage of his cousins and the rest of

the camp. Instead, he found relief and joy as everyone surrounded him.

"Let's all go to bed," Del said wearily—but
happily, as he put his arm around his cousin's shoulders. "We can get the details in the morning."

Figures slowly melted back to their fales, and
Liam, tired but somehow released, climbed the
stairs to his bed as well.

Bethany winced as soon as the screen door
slapped shut.

"I tried to stay up," Malia said groggily. "What
happened?"

"You won't believe it!" said Bethany.

The two girls whispered in the dark for another
hour and even then Bethany found it difficult to
sleep.

"What a crazy day, God," Bethany whispered.
"This has been one crazy, terrible, and wonderful
day!"

eight

The morning sun was high over the distant mountains by the time everyone began to trickle into the dining room for breakfast. As tired as they all were from the night before, there was no great rush to get to the boats.

Bethany loaded her plate high with fruit and yogurt as she struggled to wake up. Malia, the only one who did get some sleep, outdid her, piling her plate high with an impressive amount of eggs, several pieces of bacon, and some toast. Tim made pig noises as he passed their table, and Malia grinned.

"If I can't surf, I might as well eat," Malia said airily.

"Hey, check it out," Bethany whispered as all heads turned to watch Liam walk into the dining room. A weird kind of hush fell over everyone — like they were all trying to figure out what to say, if anything.

But Liam didn't look as if he had come for breakfast conversation — he looked like he had come to make an announcement. He glanced around the room and then cleared his throat. Bethany noticed that his cheeks were beginning to turn red.

"I want to tell you all," Liam began and then swallowed, "especially you, Malia and Bethany, that I am so sorry for how I acted in the water. And even out of the water. There's no excuse for what I did. And Malia, I hope you can forgive me for wrecking your surf trip."

For a moment no one said a thing. Bethany glanced at Malia and saw that her lips were trembling a little. Del and Hank looked relieved and grateful that their idiotic cousin had finally done something smart.

Then Malia walked over to Liam and gave him a hug.

Liam blushed and lowered his head. A small tear escaped from the corner of his eye, and he brushed it away quickly.

"All right, that's enough of the spotlight for you Liam!" Hank called out.

"Let's eat!" Tim said.

"Come, sit with us!" Malia added with a grin.

Liam piled his plate even higher than Malia—no small feat, but Bethany guessed his apology had allowed his appetite to return. She had been there herself, after all.

Between bites, Bethany whispered to him, "I'm sorry about your mom. That must be really hard."

Liam nodded his head, smiled weakly, and forked up another bite. He glanced shyly at Malia.

"Do you eat like that all the time?" Malia asked with a teasing grin.

"Yeah," Liam admitted with a small grin of his own. "Sometimes a lot more than this."

Bethany chuckled. "Tim has met his match!"

As soon as breakfast was out of the way, the general consensus was that it was time to get back to the business of surfing. Pod had announced that the swell had peaked overnight and returned to a playful size. A short time later, their gear was loaded and they all climbed back on the boat with Pod.

Malia was the last to climb on board. She carried a waterproof bag slung over each shoulder. One contained a video camera and the other a still camera.

Noah and Tim had made her the official photographer for the rest of the trip and had given her a crash course in how to use their equipment.

All morning long, Malia recorded the images of her friends, Liam included, getting great tube rides, floating over crashing sections, and, in the case of the younger surfers, getting some air.

That evening, Noah hooked up the camera to the camp television, and the whole crew gathered around and watched the movies and stills Malia had shot. They hooted for each good ride and laughed and played backward any wipeout.

Afterward, everyone complimented Malia on her video and photography skills.

Every day for the rest of their trip, Malia sat in the boat again, cameras ready, batteries recharged. She even bugged Pod to move his boat around so she could shoot from different angles.

Little did Noah and Tim know, but their idea to include Malia was the start of something big for her. She discovered shooting movies was not only fun but something she was good at—a fledgling filmmaker was born.

On their last day in Samoa, Bethany talked Pod into taking her and Malia out for one final surf session. She made sure it was early enough so that the adults wouldn't be there to remind Malia about doctor's orders and other precautions.

The girls watched the sun come up over the Samoan jungle and turned and smiled at each other.

"How ya feeling?" Bethany asked.

Malia laughed. "After that sunrise? Great! I thought the salt water would sting some of my cuts, but they must be healed enough to handle!"

They threw their boards in the water and dived in. Bethany broke the surface and waited for Malia to come up.

"Okay. Here's my gift to you: You can have any wave you want today!"

"In that case, I want them all!"

"Don't be a wave hog!"

Malia started snorting and paddled for an oncoming wave at the same time. She was still snorting like a pig as she sailed past Bethany.

Bethany laughed, wishing she could've taped Malia like that—somehow freeze-frame the moment forever. It would be another memory of Samoa that she would keep in her heart for the rest of her life.

The flight back to Hawaii was scheduled to leave midafternoon. Del, Hank, and Liam were outbound on a ten p.m. flight.

After lunch, the Hamilton family busied themselves unscrewing fins, loading board bags, and packing up their gear.

Tagiilima trotted back and forth with surfboards, stacking them high on the rusty roof racks of the surf-camp van.

Bethany strolled into the dining room to find it crowded with people from the village. Pastor Samuel was there and explained that the people in their village had never met a celebrity before—could they get her autograph to remember her by?

Bethany was a little embarrassed—but she was touched. The Samoans were such a kind, gentle people, and she would miss them. She accepted the marker that was offered to her by a little girl and in her loose scrawl signed papers, napkins, magazines, T-shirts, and even kids' arms with her name and a verse.

Tagiilima tapped his watch, and Pastor Samuel said something to the crowd, which caused them to leave, waving as they went.

Liam, Del, and Hank each gave the Hamiltons a heart-filled good-bye, and everyone exchanged addresses and emails.

Bethany gave Liam her Bible. "I have others at home."

Soon the camp van was bouncing down the narrow road with each passenger staring out in silent reflection of their adventures over the last two weeks.

At the airport, one last strange thing happened—Tagiilima cried.

"I sorry, I sorry," he said. "I drive surfers many times, but you are special. You make me feel like your family." He misted up again.

Tom, in particular, was deeply touched. As they parted, Tom shook his hand vigorously and gave him all the Samoan talas he had in his pocket as a tip. It was a generous tip.

Bethany hugged him, and he hugged her back—a big bear of a hug that left her breathless ... and a little misty-eyed herself.

As the long flight to Hawaii got underway, Noah and Tim fiddled with the onboard movie selection. Tom and Cheri fell asleep in each other's arms like a couple of high school sweethearts.

Bethany dug deep into her backpack and got out a blank journal and a pencil.

"What are you doing?" Malia asked.

Bethany looked up. "Schoolwork. My assignment is to write about this trip, and I thought I'd write down some stuff while it's still fresh in my mind."

"Have a blast!" Malia said as she plugged her headset into the armrest and started searching through the selections.

When she turned to look at Bethany, Malia saw that she had written two lines before she tilted her head back and fell asleep. The pencil rested on Bethany's open journal.

Malia took a little peek at what Bethany had penned.

"I never imagined I would see God work so much good through people on a surf trip—and I'm pretty good at imagining stuff. Now that I think of it, God has a pretty awesome imagination himself. The best!"

nine

"You know what's the worst thing about surfing in California?" Malia asked Bethany.

In unison they shouted, "Wet suits!"

"I can't feel my feet," Bethany laughed. "Are these my toes, or are they popsicles?"

"I *told* you to wear booties."

Late fall found the girls sitting in the dark blue water of Crystal Pier in San Diego, California. The morning fog had burned off, and the sun was just starting to bathe the beach in warmth.

"We've got time for one more wave before we have to be back," Bethany said, shivering a little as she silently prayed for the sun to hurry up.

"Fee-fi-fo-fum, I feel a set is about to come," a voice came from somewhere behind them. They both turned to see Liam grinning at them.

"Do you have a sixth sense about waves, Liam?" Malia asked, and Liam's grin got wider.

"No, it's just that this is my home break, and I have it kinda dialed. I can tell that something is coming. Don't ask me how."

"Uh, could it be your cousin Del up on the pier who's waving his arms frantically and pointing to the horizon?" Bethany said, beginning to laugh.

"Oh, is he up there doing that?" Liam's brows raised in mock surprise. "See, I do have a gift!" Liam noticed the "oh, really?" look on their faces and conceded. "Okay, okay. What you gotta do is look for the waves that angle in through the pier. They're the ones that have the long ride. The ones that come straight through tend to close out. It's all about sandbar here."

"Got it!" Bethany said with a wink to Malia.

The bump on the horizon soon appeared, and the girls followed Liam to the takeoff spot right next to a barnacle-encrusted piling.

The swell racing to the beach swept through the pier at a slight angle, producing the very wave that Liam had talked about.

"Go, Bethany! Go!" Liam shouted.

"But you're in the takeoff spot," Bethany protested.

"So what! Just go!"

Bethany took a few strokes and dropped down the glassy face of a perfectly shaped wave. Putting her skills into full throttle, she tore into the wave with arching turns and slashing cutbacks, and ended at the beach with a 360 air.

From the sand at the top of the pier, cameras clicked.

"This one is yours, Malia!" Liam shouted.

Malia smiled and nodded her head in thanks to Liam. Then she spun her board around and within several paddles she was sailing into action, charging down the line using her speed to demolish the smooth, deep-blue wave.

Bethany watched her friend surf from the shoreline and waited for her to end her ride next to her.

Both girls peeled off their leashes, wrapped them around their boards and headed toward the sand.

They got no more than a dozen feet or so when a mob of reporters and camera operators advanced through the soft wet sand, thrusting microphones in their faces.

"It's remarkable that a local event would attract a celebrity like you," a reporter said, pushing his mike toward Bethany. "What made you come?"

"Well, we were invited by a friend. And when we heard about what he was trying to do, we knew we had to be here," Bethany said.

"And just how did you get the idea to give handicapped kids the opportunity to surf? Was it because of your own handicap?" another reporter asked.

"I have a handicap?" Bethany grinned. "Where?" A few of the reporters laughed, and she glanced behind her. "Actually, you should talk to the brains behind this. Where is Liam?"

Liam had quietly walked behind the girls. His blond hair jetted off in different directions, and his skinny frame looked a bit more bulky in the thick wet suit. Bethany couldn't help thinking he looked better somehow than the first time she met him. More confident, maybe. She smiled at him as the cameras and microphones turned his way.

"Are you the one who organized this terrific event?"

"Well, not just me," Liam answered honestly. "There are a lot of people who help to make something like this happen. People who really know how to organize—people who helped sponsor us. I just kinda came up with the idea and other people took it from there."

"Can you tell us how the idea came about?" another reporter asked.

"I got the idea after a trip to Samoa," Liam said, glancing towards Bethany and Malia. "It just occurred to me that the fun of surfing was something that should be given to others to enjoy too. Not long after I came home, I saw a kid in a wheelchair and I said to myself, 'That kid will never surf.' And then I got to thinking, 'Why not?' Then one thing led to another, and here we are."

Liam paused for a second and then said, "Ya gotta excuse me. We're going to start up things in a few minutes."

As Liam, Bethany, and Malia made their way up from the water's edge, they could hear the news reporter speaking into her microphone: "We are here in San Diego, California, where a young surfer decided to give the *stoke* of surfing to young people who might never have a chance to experience it. He has managed to gather professional surfers from all around the country, including Bethany Hamilton from Hawaii, to be part of the surf clinic for kids with handicaps. Surf companies from all over have donated equipment, and clothing companies have made sure that every kid who gets in the water today goes home looking like a surfer as well."

On the sand a huge stage was set up. Banners and flags sagged, waiting for the afternoon wind to inflate them. A Christian rock band was setting up their gear, and volunteers were putting the final touches on a huge table of giveaways for the kids.

"How did you pull this off?" Bethany asked Liam as she looked around with amazement.

"Actually, my dad helped a lot," Liam said. "He doesn't surf at all, but he loves to organize stuff. When I suggested the idea to him, it fired him up. Besides, he's got plenty of money and pull. He got Del and Hank involved too. They know lots and lots of people in the surf industry. Most of the free goodies and gear came because of their hookups."

"Well, it's awesome. A really great idea," Bethany said.

"That's what happens when you put your faith into action," Malia added.

"I dunno. It's just fun," Liam said shyly, then he glanced up at them. "In fact, you wanna know something? I have had more fun putting this together than I have from even the best wave I've surfed."

"That's 'cause it's not about you. It always works that way," Bethany said with a smile.

"Well, let's go teach some kids to surf!" said Liam.

For the rest of the morning, large foam surfboards were loaded with handicapped kids, some of whom had to be carried to the water by teams of men. Each child was geared up in a loaner wet suit, courtesy of a famous wet-suit maker.

Guided into the surf on both sides by a whole army of volunteers, including Bethany and Malia, the kids shivered in the cold water in spite of their wet suits. When the first wave rolled in, a volunteer would slide up behind the child and hold on tightly to keep him or her from slipping off the board when the white water hit.

Squeals of delight erupted as the huge foamy surfboard was launched by the wave and the pair rode all the way to the sand.

Depending on the nature of their handicap, some children belly rode in. Others, in time, made the journey to the beach with a wide stinkbug stance.

"Do it again! Do it again!" the kids yelled delightedly.

Parents waded in to take photos of their children riding a surfboard for the first time. The whole experience filled everyone with a joy they couldn't explain, but felt deeply.

At the end of the morning, a van pulled up and for the next five minutes pizzas were unloaded and taken down to the beach. Huge ice chests were rolled out and the children and parents feasted happily on the sand.

"I'm worn out from chasing kids," Bethany said, tired but happy.

"Me too," Malia said.

"Me *three*," Liam admitted, and they laughed.

"And I'm hungry," Bethany added.

"Help yourself to the pizza," Liam said, "but leave some room for dinner—we have a special surprise for you!"

By the end of the afternoon the kids were very tired. All of them were wet, salty, and sandy as they made their way back to their family cars with huge smiles on their faces. Their arms bulged with T-shirts, stickers, hats, and other goodies. Most kids had three or four helium balloons tied to their wrists.

Bethany guessed that on the way home ninety percent of the kids would try to convince their parents to buy them a surfboard.

That's how surfing works, she thought with a grin. *Try it once and you are hooked for life.*

Liam dropped the girls off at the house where they were staying and said, "You need to be ready by six thirty p.m. My dad and I will pick you up for dinner."

"Oh great!" Bethany laughed. "Now Malia and I will have to fight over who gets the bathroom first!"

Good to his word, Liam arrived at six thirty, and they all piled into his dad's huge SUV with Bethany apologizing that her hair was still wet. Malia had won the first round for the bathroom.

Dinner was at the Fish Grotto, where the girls were invited to select a lobster for dinner out of a huge tank in the middle of the room.

All was going fine until Bethany decided to name the lobster that Malia picked. Malia decided right then she couldn't eat it.

"How can you eat something that you've named?" she complained.

Everyone laughed at her for her sensitivity to lobsters.

Finally Malia settled for a fish, but insisted that she not meet the creature before it was lying grilled on her plate.

"Mr. MacLeod, thank you for bringing us over for this event," Bethany said to Liam's dad.

"You can call me Frank," he said with a smile. "And you are very welcome. All I have heard about for months is Bethany and Malia, Malia and Bethany." His smile broadened. "I figured this was as good a way as any to have the chance to meet you two."

Both Bethany and Malia blushed. Mr. MacLeod leaned forward. "And I wanted to thank you too."

Both girls looked at each other, puzzled. Liam's dad cleared his throat.

"When Liam came home, there was something different about him," he explained. "At first, I couldn't figure it out. After all, he had only gone on a surf trip. But after a while he started going to a church group and getting really involved."

The older man stared off for a moment, then looked at Liam and the girls.

"I never told my family, but when I was younger, I was an active churchgoer as well. Then life got busy, my job took off, and, well, let's just say somewhere along the line ... my faith got lost."

He managed to smile again.

"But when I saw the new sparkle in my son, it reminded me of what I once had and I guess I figured that it was about time to get it back. So I started following Liam to church, and I am happy to say that I rediscovered the faith that was lost."

Bethany and Malia were thrilled. They had never imagined that the ripple effect of the events in Samoa would reach from one teenager, to his dad, to hundreds of kids who were given a chance to surf.

"That's really cool," Bethany said softly to Mr. MacLeod. But she wanted to stand on the table in the crowded restaurant and yell, "Woo-hoo! Thank you, God!"

The fog had rolled back in by the time Mr. MacLeod dropped the girls off at the home where they were staying.

Before they got out of the car, Liam reached down and produced a taped-up box.

"Bethany, I meant to send this to you, but then when I knew that you were coming here, I decided to wait and hand deliver it."

"What is it?"

"I don't know," Liam said with a shrug. "I mean, it isn't from me. It's from Tagiilima. He asked me to make sure to give it to you. I guess he thinks that the United States is small and cozy like Samoa and that I would bump into you at the market or something."

Bethany laughed. "Oh, okay, thanks for delivering it, Liam. Thanks for everything."

The day, which had been nice and warm, had given over to the chilly coastal air that both girls claimed to love if for no other reason than it gave them the chance to wear sweaters and jackets that they never used in Hawaii.

Rather than go into the house, the girls decided to sit on the front steps for a while. "What's that weird smell?" Malia said suddenly, glancing around.

"That's a skunk! You've never smelled a skunk before?"

"Duh? Are you forgetting that we don't have skunks in Hawaii?"

"Oh, yeah!" Bethany laughed. "Well, it's probably far away; if it were nearer we couldn't stand to sit outside. It'll fade in a little bit."

"Good. I like sitting out here."

The girls sat in silence for a few moments, then Bethany said, "What a strange past few months this has been. What do they call it? A chain of events?"

"Yeah," said Malia. "Who could have imagined that all this would have happened?"

"I can tell you that I would have never guessed it on the way to the hospital with you," Bethany admitted.

"And I would never have guessed it when I was bouncing on the reef in Samoa!" Malia said with a laugh. "I guess it really is true that 'all things work together for good for those who love God.'"

"Yes," Bethany said as she smiled. "It really is true."

"Well, I guess we prove that," said Malia.

"Without a doubt."

The girls sat quietly looking at the fog dance around the streetlights when Bethany suddenly remembered the box she had been given.

"Let's see what's in here!" she said, running to get it.

The box was well sealed, but Bethany was able to use her nails to dig her way through the tape. Undoing the wrapping, she found a neatly folded mat. As Bethany unfolded it she saw that it was trimmed with brightly colored feathers.

"Oh, my gosh, do you know what this is?"

"A repentance mat!" they both said at the same time. Then Bethany noticed the picture at the bottom of the box, along with a letter.

Tagiilima smiled back at her from the picture, his arm wrapped around a beautiful little girl who was holding a tattered *People* magazine in her hands as they sat on the beach.

"No way," Bethany whispered.

"That's the little girl from the church!" Malia said excitedly.

Bethany turned to the note, written in simple print and painstakingly neat:

> *Miss Bethany, I send you this repentance mat to thank you. And to tell you that because of your words I no longer need to be under it. I too lost my wife and had much anger. Like Mr. Liam. But no more. When Jesus lifted the mat off me, he lifted my burden.*

"Bethany, look!" Malia said suddenly as she pointed to the picture again — but more specifically to Tagiilima's bare foot ... and his missing *big toe*. "We must have been so busy surfing we never noticed before."

"So that was Tagiilima under the repentance mat at Pastor Samuel's!" Bethany said as a chill went up her spine.

"Not anymore," Malia said. Bethany felt a sudden rush of tears well up in her eyes. She was amazed and overwhelmed beyond words.

She glanced down at the place where her arm had been and thought of all the ways God had used her since the tragedy. She had believed she was going to Samoa to surf—but God had so much more planned. Not just for her but for all the lives he had touched through her.

"God works in all things, Malia," Bethany said as a tear escaped and ran down her cheek.

"Yeah," Malia said, brushing away her own tears. "It's pretty awesome, isn't it?"

Soul Surfer Series

Storm
a novel

CHECK OUT this excerpt from book three in the Soul Surfer Series

written by *Rick Bundschuh*
inspired by *Bethany Hamilton*

"My lungs are going to collapse!" Holly Silva gasped as she melted into a human puddle on the park grass. "I can't believe you talked me into this!"

"You're welcome," Bethany panted as she landed next to Holly with a grin. She never got tired of running at Hanalei Bay. Surrounded by towering green cliffs and waterfalls that seemed to go on forever, it was like having a running trail in the middle of Jurassic Park. Minus the man-eating dinosaurs, of course.

The run had been good for her, she thought, glancing up at the wide blue bowl of sky. Good enough to shake off the cloud that had been looming over her ever since waking from that crazy dream.

"How many miles was that?"

Bethany glanced over as Holly threw her arms wide across the grass. Bethany smiled. The cool thing about hanging with Holly was you couldn't stay in a weird mood for long.

"Miles? More like one mile," Bethany said, and then laughed as Holly's green eyes widened in disbelief. "It's running in the sand that gets you."

"It's running in the sand *after* surfing all morning. No wonder Malia and Jenna bailed on us!"

"Malia and Jenna aren't as gullible as you," Bethany teased. Bethany had to bite her lip to keep from giggling as her friend sat up. Holly's short brown hair was dark with sweat and sticking up all over the place.

"It's winter training, Holly," Bethany continued when she was able to talk without laughing. "You'll be glad you did it with me when you survive Hanalei Bay when it's fifteen feet."

"News flash, Bethany; I don't like to surf when it's fifteen feet—*you* like to surf when it's fifteen feet!" Holly narrowed her eyes. "And why do you keep looking at my hair?"

"Well ..." Bethany burst out laughing. "It's a little scary."

"Ugh," Holly groaned, running her hands through her hair as her eyes darted toward the cute surfers tossing a Frisbee on the beach. "That's what I get for following you around the bay twice!"

Bethany smiled as she turned her gaze towards the rocky shoreline on the other side of the bay. Suddenly, her smile faded a little and she felt a shiver go up her back. Why couldn't she shake that dream? *There was something about those rocks—*

"So, tell me why you like torturing yourself like this." Holly said, interrupting Bethany's thoughts.

Bethany leaned back in the grass and thought for a moment. "Remember last January at the Big Surf?"

"I remember you were the only girl crazy enough to go out."

"Well, I got caught by flat rock in a cleanup set. I was pinned to the bottom for the first wave, rolled around by the second, and finally broke surface for a breath after the third wave—"

"Exactly *why* I don't surf the bay when it's fifteen feet!"

"No, you don't get it! What I'm saying is, I was a little freaked out—but not like I would've been if I hadn't trained. If you *know* you can handle a couple of wave hold downs, then it isn't as scary..." Bethany's voice trailed off as she thought about the dream again, and she wondered if it meant that she needed to train harder—be better prepared.

She glanced over at Holly who was quiet for once, with a thoughtful look on her face as she studied the sky. Bethany wished Holly would say something—anything—to lighten the mood.

"Hello?"

"I was just trying to figure out what's worse," Holly said finally, her grin reappearing. "Training with you or being wiped out by a massive wave."

"Very funny."

"I gotta get up and find something to drink," Holly laughed, then groaned as she slowly rose to her feet. "My body hates me, and we still have the car wash to do!"

"Let's head into town. I'll buy you a bottle of water for being such a good sport," Bethany offered.

Holly arched a brow at her. "Good sport?"

"Okay . . . for running with me!" Bethany added. They both laughed.

"Ready to stagger to the store?" asked Holly.

"You stagger, I kinda feel like jogging."

"Bethany, you are such a show-off!"

Bethany grinned, feeling her spirits rise. "Catch up, and I'll let you in on an idea I have for the car wash!"

"I'm probably going to regret this!" Holly called out and then ran to catch up.

They were guzzling water in front of the Big Save grocery store when Bethany's mom arrived to shuttle them to the church car wash.

"I don't know how you girls do it," Cheri said as they scrambled into the van. "I have a hard time keeping up as the driver!"

"You reap what you sow, Mom. Isn't that what you always tell me?"

"Hmm." Cheri pursed her lips in thought as she backed out of the parking space. "I wonder what the wash-me bandits are going to reap?"

She grinned at Holly in the rearview mirror. "Any ideas?"

Holly blushed, but Bethany burst out laughing. Her mom had spotted all the dirty rear windows they had written *wash me* on as they headed into town.

"We'll reap business for the car wash—for the mission trip."

"So we can go build homes in Mexico for those less fortunate." Holly added with a hopeful grin.

"Uh, huh," Cheri said and then did a double take in the rearview mirror. "Okay, how did you two manage to get *my* back window without me noticing?"

Cheri shook her head in amazement, and Bethany and Holly broke into a fresh round of laughter.

"Is this the third or fourth car wash?" Holly asked once she caught her breath.

"Third," Bethany said, glancing over the seat. "I just wish there was something else we could do. It feels like it's taking forever, and I've been dying to go on a mission trip since I was little!"

"Too bad we're not *trustafarians*."

"What?" Bethany and her mom said at the same time and then laughed.

Holly grinned. "You know, hippies with Rastafarian hair who live in the jungle and only come into town to get money out of their trust fund accounts. *Trust-afarians*. Get it?"

Bethany and her mom groaned. Holly was almost famous for the crazy way she described people. If she didn't know of a term, she was happy to make one up.

"Check it out," Holly said, suddenly pointing to the side passenger window. Bethany turned in time to see a long black limousine in the lane next to them. "*They* should be at our fundraiser!"

"No doubt," Bethany said slowly as she watched the limo pick up speed to pass them. She was suddenly caught off guard as the face of a teenage girl turned to stare back at them. She was pretty in a polished kind of way, with dark hair cut in a shiny bob and fair skin. The girl noticed them watching her and quickly looked away.

"Probably a *celebutante*," Holly added knowingly.

Bethany grinned and shook her head just as the girl glanced up to the sky. Bethany was struck hard by the sad look on the girl's face.

I wonder what it is that's made her so sad?

Something about the girl tugged at Bethany — something she couldn't put her finger on — like the way her eyes kept being drawn back to the rocks at Hanalei Bay. Like her dream.

It wasn't that she thought people with money couldn't have problems. Her friend Liam and his dad had been through some really bad stuff — until they found God. Even now, they still dealt with the same things everyone worried about, prayed about. But what if someone didn't know God? What if what they owned was all they thought they had?

"Is that it?" Andrea looked out the window of the limousine to the west as an awesome view of towering cliffs with waterfalls free-falling down to a slip of white sand and ocean opened up before them. Colorado had some cool-looking mountains, she thought, but *nothing* like this.

"Yeah, that's it, kiddo."

Andrea turned around, surprised at the hint of excitement she thought she heard in her mom's voice. Her mom glanced up from the map she'd been squinting at and smiled—a smile that Andrea couldn't ever remember seeing before. For a moment, she almost looked and sounded kind of young.

Maybe. She tried not to hope too much, but she yearned to have a real family that hung out together. She thought of the blonde girl she'd seen in the van, hair blowing in the wind, with such a huge smile on her face. The lady driving had the same kind of smile. They looked like they were having fun together.

Andrea looked across the seat to where her dad sat. She saw that he was looking toward the cliffs too. She almost reached out to grab his hand. Something about the way he looked reminded her of herself; sad and alone, even in a car full of people. *I wonder if he's thinking about Uncle Mike?*

Andrea glanced at her brother. He was sprawled out on the seat next to her as he nodded along with whatever was playing on his iPod. Mark drove her crazy most of the time, but she couldn't imagine what it would be like without him. "One day he's there, and the next he's just … gone," she'd heard her dad say with a shaky voice the night he got the call about Uncle Mike.

He'd said it like it couldn't be real. It wasn't real to her, either. Her uncle was gone. Gone where?

Andrea leaned her head against the car window and glanced up to the blue expanse of sky again, searching. She'd never really thought about that kind of stuff until now—she knew for sure her mom and dad hadn't.

Her dad's mantra had always been if something was lost or broken, you opened your wallet and bought a replacement—or had it fixed.

But people can't be replaced, Andrea thought, curling her legs under her as she stared at the sky. And she'd never heard of anyone that could fix a broken heart.

Body and Soul

A Girl's Guide to a Fit, Fun and Fabulous Life

Bethany Hamilton
with Dustin Dillberg

Bethany Hamilton has become a fitness expert by virtue of being a professional athlete who has excelled—and she's done it while overcoming incredible challenges. In *Body & Soul*, a total wellness book for girls ages 8 and up, Bethany shares some of her own experiences while helping young girls gain confidence and develop a pattern of healthy living starting at a young age. In addition to workouts and recipes, Bethany also shares her unstoppable faith and emphasizes how spiritual health is just as important as physical health.

Includes:

- Workouts specially developed for young girls by Bethany's personal trainer
- Recipes and information on healthy eating based on "Bethany's food pyramid," which follows the Mediterranean diet
- Advice on deepening your spiritual health and total body wellness

Available in stores and online!

Soul Surfer Series

Clash

Rick Bundschuh, Inspired by Bethany Hamilton

Book one in the Soul Surfer Series

Burned

Rick Bundschuh, Inspired by Bethany Hamilton

Book two in the Soul Surfer Series

Storm

Rick Bundschuh, Inspired by Bethany Hamilton

Book three in the Soul Surfer Series

Crunch

Rick Bundschuh, Inspired by Bethany Hamilton

Book four in the Soul Surfer Series

Available in stores and online!